J.T. Cheyanne

Just Jordan

J.T. Cheyanne

~ * ~ * ~ * ~

Copyright © J.T. Cheyanne, 2020
First Edition February 2020
Published by: Lachi Publications
ISBN: 978-0-9899725-8-1

Cover design by Tracey Weston
~ * ~ * ~ * ~

This book is a work of fiction. Names, characters, places and incidents are either the product of the author's imagination or are used fictitiously, and any resemblance to any actual persons, living or dead, events, or locales is entirely coincidental.

J.T. Cheyanne

DEDICATION

For my son, Devan Trey and his wife, Ashton Jordan - a different take on your love story. So glad the two of you, Daniel and Dakota and Shannon understand my craziness. Love all of you and my sweet and sassy grandbabies, Hadley, Averi and Declan.

~ * ~ * ~ * ~

Chapter One
~*~*~

"I'm not going back there, and that's the end of it. Just drop it, Silas."

"But, it's great publicity. A small-town boy who made the big show returns home and donates a cool mil to the local high school where he started. It's movie script perfect."

Trey finished his fourth set of reps and dropped the loaded barbell to the floor. The familiar clank of metal against metal filled the room. "Who says I have a million dollars to toss around? My contract's up for renewal this year."

Silas Barton, his long-time agent slash publicist, waved away the comment. "I'm working on that. The Wildcats aren't going to chance losing the best quarterback in the league."

Trey adjusted the weights on the bench press and settled onto the bench. "Spot," he grumbled and laid back. "A quarterback who's getting older. Have you seen what's coming out of the college level?"

When Silas merely grunted, Trey closed his fingers around the iron bar and took a deep breath. He heaved the weight off of the brackets and began the rhythmic up and down. To his credit, Silas took his spotting duties seriously. His bright grey eyes watched Trey for any slip or falter. The agent was protecting his asset with eagle-eyed sharpness. No harming the merchandise.

Trey knew he was being unfair. Silas was a friend, not just his agent. It was the thought of Avery, Wyoming that twisted in his gut and triggered his jaded outlook. Twenty years since he'd left the small town on a football scholarship. Four years at university, sixteen in the pros. He wasn't washed up. Yet. But, the time was inching closer.

The barbell hit the brackets. Trey concentrated on breathing before the next set of reps. For once, Silas kept his own counsel. That lasted until Trey hit the third set.

"The fans would love it. The league could use the good press for a change, and the Wildcats can't ignore a fan favorite. Your merch is through the roof. Just your jersey sales for last month were enough to pay for that fancy penthouse of yours for the rest of the year."

"It's September, Si, and it was pre-season. The sales will go down," Trey grunted as he shifted the weights back to the bar and sat up.

"You know what I mean, asshat." Free of spotting duty, Silas snagged a towel and tossed it to Trey before slouching against the wall. "Those figures don't even touch your endorsements. Companies love athletes who support charities, especially children. We could increase your portfolio. You should really think about it."

Trey grimaced. "Just when am I supposed to find time for a class reunion? That's week eight in the season, about midway through. You know how hectic it is then. And, it's a Thursday night game. In New York. The reunion is Saturday night. In Wyoming. I'm scheduled for a one-on-one with ESPN on Sunday and The Team is scheduled for Make-A-Wish visits at St. Jude's on Monday."

When Silas grinned, Trey knew he'd screwed up. His little outburst told Silas that he had given it some thought, had actually taken the time to check a calendar.

"I'll get the team jet to fly you out to Wyoming and back. We can leave after the game on Thursday night, hit the pep rally on Friday and then the reunion on Saturday. We can fly back out Sunday morning and be in New York in time for the interview. It's scheduled for the evening sweeps anyway. You've operated on less sleep before, and the following game is a home game so very little travel time. You'll have a week to recuperate."

"Oh yeah, in between my training schedule, practice, team meetings and endorsement appointments."

Silas grinned. "You chose this life, big guy. And, you chose me. I'm just trying to make us both some money."

Trey snorted. "Sounds to me like you're trying to give it away. You want me to donate that much to the high school, you get it okay-ed by my accountant."

Silas shuddered but grinned. Trey rolled his eyes and moved to the leg press. Of course, the agent was happy; he was getting what he wanted. Trey Bright was headed home to the minuscule dot on the map that was Avery, Wyoming.

As much as he didn't want to go, Silas had never led him astray before. If the man said it was a good career move, fine. And, if his heart beat just a little faster, well that didn't have anything to do with the past. It wasn't every day a fella just handed over a million dollars.

Trey adjusted the weights on the leg press and settled into position. "I'll leave it to you and Ms. Metcalf to decide the exact amount I can donate. I am not tangling with her."

"Chicken."

"Damn right, and you're matching ten percent of what I donate."

"Wait, what?" Silas looked up from his cell phone where he had been busily texting, probably the team about a jet.

"It's either matching, or you're bringing your ass with me to Avery. There's not a damn thing to do there except stare at four walls and pray for the departure date."

And, that wasn't fair to Avery. He'd loved growing up in the small community where everyone knew your parents and remembered your birthday. Where Fourth of July fireworks and Christmas pageants at church were tradition. Where small-town Americana thrived in the mom and pop diner, the locally owned drug store, and the corner auto shop that had been run by the same family for seventy-five years.

There was one reason he didn't want to go back to Wyoming. Trey rubbed a hand over the sudden tightness in his chest that had nothing to do with weight lifting and a lot to do with the mom and pop scenario.

"How about I match five percent and go with you? Best of both?"

Trey snorted in laughter before he realized Silas was serious. "It's that important to you that I go? You'd risk being out of action?"

"Not a lot of action to be missed in one weekend, unless you've heard rumors I haven't." Silas shrugged. "Be interesting to see where you came from; meet your extended family. The stories your mom and dad tell sound fantastic to an only child, city sewer rat."

Trey laughed again. "I do not see you as the backwoods, small town, bumpkin type. In fact, I'm not sure I've ever seen you in anything but a perfectly matched and fitted suit."

"I have blue jeans and tee shirts. Somewhere." Silas flashed a quick grin, but it didn't hide the pain that flickered in his steel grey eyes. "So, that means we're going, right? It's a deal."

Trey shook his head and sighed. "I thought we'd already determined that. I'm going back for you, Silas. Just for you, so, if anything goes wrong. It's on you."

"What can go wrong in Avery?"

Everything. But, he couldn't tell Silas that so Trey ducked his head, choosing the safe out. "Just sayin'. This bad idea is all yours."

Chapter Two
~ * ~ * ~

"The reunion is next weekend. Do you think he'll come home?"

"Would you?"

"And lord it over all of Avery, Wyoming? Hell yes!" Janice Meeks shoved her long blond braid back over her shoulder. "He got out just like he said he would. Everyone in America knows his name. He's all over TV in those underwear and soda commercials. He's probably rolling in money."

"Which is why he definitely doesn't want to come back to Avery. There's nothing for him here."

Jordan Brooks broke eye contact with his best friend, shoved his glasses back up onto his nose and focused on his task. With great precision, he plated the bacon double cheeseburger next to the basket of curly fries and slid the entire thing across the small counter to Janice. "Order up."

Eyes the color of warm caramel narrowed. Pretty pink-tinted lips turned down at the corners. "Jordan...."

"No!" Jordan's raised voice not only interrupted her; it drew every gaze in the crowded diner. Lunch was the busiest time for The Table Top especially on college game day Saturdays when his dad fired up the grill out back and smoked ribs and Boston butts for pulled pork sandwiches. The games would be on the big screens and cheers and groans would punctuate the televised announcers.

Except, his dad wasn't out back with the grill. He was at home recovering from the stroke. So, Jordan was filling in as a fry cook and grill master instead of grading math tests at home for his regular day job as a high school teacher. Janice glared at him, snatched the plate from the counter and stalked off. Jordan sighed and turned his back on the stares of his neighbors and friends.

"Everything okay?"

Jordan forced a smile and turned around. "Yes, Mom. Got careless and bumped against the grill. I think I'm out of practice. You talked to dad?"

"That wasn't a burn yell, young man, and your dad is fine. What did Janice say this time? I swear that girl has no filter. I don't know how the two of you get along."

"I have enough filter for both of us." He leaned down and kissed his mom's cheek as she came closer. "She keeps me from being boring, and I keep her out of trouble."

"I am not arguing with that. She's a danger to herself."

"Better than a danger to others." He scowled. "Hey wait! Are you agreeing that I'm boring?"

Tavia Brooks laughed and reached across him to take the spatula. She bumped her hip against his. "I never said any such thing. Go see if the first butt is ready. The Lion's Club is coming in at twelve-thirty and they all ordered ahead."

Jordan gasped dramatically and clutched his chest. "You do think I'm boring! My own mother! How will I survive?"

He caught the dishrag she tossed at him and winked at her as he slipped out the kitchen and into the office. As soon as the door clicked closed behind him, the smile dropped from his face. Janice's question played in his head.

Did he think Trey Bright would come back for the reunion? That answer was easy. Not in a million years. Did he want Trey to come back? That answer was much more complicated. Twenty-one years ago, Trey had become the center of Jordan's sheltered world.

Shrugging into his coat, he exited the office and hurried outside to the grill. It was chilly for October, but the grill provided some warmth as he drew closer. Smoke curled from the vent giving the air a delectable scent. They were the only diner in the state that offered authentic Southern barbeque.

His dad, Dan Brooks, had been born and raised in southern Alabama. While stationed at Warren Air Force Base, he'd met and married Tavia Douglas. After his discharge, they returned to Avery, her hometown, and took over the diner from her parents. Jordan had never stepped foot in Alabama. Avery was all he knew.

Jordan lifted the top of the grill. The familiar sound of sizzling meat filled his ears. He'd grown up at the diner while his parents worked. So many weekends, he'd spent in the same spot, learning the recipe for the sauce, the exact blend of the rub for the meat, the heat of the grill chasing away the chilly mornings and afternoons. The back of the diner was also the first place Trey had ever spoken to him.

He wasn't going to think about Trey. It was fruitless. Damn Janice and her questions. Jordan closed the grill and backed away from it. There was no way Trey Bright was coming back to Avery, not for a reunion or any other reason. He knew how much Trey had wanted to leave, and he knew better than anyone why Trey would never come back.

Chapter Three
~ * ~ * ~

Sprawled in a chair in front of an unlit fireplace in the Jackson Hole Airport, Trey struggled to ignore the chatter as the two man film crew claimed their luggage and equipment. Silas had hired the crew to film the entire visit to Avery. He should have known Silas was going to make a huge production of the situation. The agent never missed an opportunity to shed positive publicity on his clients. Whether they wanted it or not. And, Trey definitely didn't want it. Not here; not in Avery; not even in Wyoming.

The game had been brutal. Joints ached; muscles bordered on cramps and his stomach felt like Mike Tyson's favorite punching bag. Climbing immediately into an airplane and sitting still for three hours hadn't been the greatest decision. He was stiff, sore and grumpy. And, he was in the last place he wanted to be. Ever.

Trey shifted positions and bit back a curse. He refused to take his bad mood out on the two guys. It wasn't their fault he was stuck in a chair too small for his large frame, hours away from a place that had nearly ripped him apart at the seams.

He cracked an eye to see what progress, if any, was being made. It still looked like chaos to him. He snapped his lid closed and sighed. His lone duffel bag emblazoned with the Wildcats logo had been claimed easily enough and served as a foot prop. It contained one suit, a few pair of underwear, sweats for the return flight and his toiletries. He didn't plan to be in Avery any longer than he had to be. Silas had either missed that memo or was ignoring it. For the moment.

Inevitably, his thoughts drifted to his last visit to Jackson Hole. There had been a small film crew then, too. The local TV station caught his departure, his mother's tears and his father's beaming smile. It aired on the local nightly news, small potatoes in the wide scheme of world news, but huge in the small city of Avery.

He had been out of sorts that day, too, despite it being his big day. It was the fulfillment of a dream. Big Ten football scholarship, escape from Avery, a college education and a chance at the pros. Yet, everything paled because one thing, rather, one person, had been missing. The one person who mattered the most.

Jordan.

Trey had known he was gay since elementary school. While the other boys were whispering about girls and "going steady", he'd hidden his feelings behind his love of football. At eighteen, he hadn't been ready to acknowledge that part of himself. On the cusp of getting everything he'd worked for since first strapping on a helmet back in the Pop Warner league, he'd maintained his silence with everyone. Except Jordan.

When it was time for Trey to go, Jordan had said he understood. They made plans. Things would get better, but first, he had to leave. Alone. So, he'd pasted on a smile, hugged his momma and climbed aboard the plane despite the gut-churning unease that had threatened to choke him.

Trey sat up abruptly and scrubbed a hand over his face. Before the damned reunion invitation arrived in the mail, he hadn't allowed himself to examine his feelings or dwell on memories of Jordan. It hurt too much. He'd banished Jordan and the idea of love to the darkest recesses of his mind. He had to out of sheer self-preservation. With the lid pried off by a thin piece of stationary, his stomach twisted in a knot. His palms were sweaty and his heart felt like a snare drum.

Trey surged to his feet and grabbed the duffel. What the hell was he thinking? He'd sworn he would never return to Avery. Two decades later, he still had no desire to face the memories. He didn't think he ever would be. He looked around for Silas. Surely, the plane could just turn around and head back to New York. He could mail a check. It was still a donation. It still counted. The reunion was a bad idea.

"We're staying in Jackson tonight so you can get some shut-eye. We'll head out to Avery in the morning." Silas appeared on his left side, snagged the handles of the duffel bag and yanked. "The film crew headed outside to load the equipment into the rental. You ready?"

No. It hovered on the tip of his tongue. Silas lifted an eyebrow in question. Trey opened his mouth, but the denial didn't come out.

"Yeah, sure." He hoped Silas attributed the lack of enthusiasm to the rough game and long flight. He didn't need or want the agent asking too many questions.

"Those Viper linebackers had your number, eh?"

Trey shrugged. "Just one of those games. Their defense was clicking on all cylinders." He forced a smile. "But, no match for our offense. Long as we get the W, it's all good."

"And good for our paychecks." Silas pushed his way out of the airport and climbed into the loaded SUV. "Speaking of, I have the new contract in my computer bag if you want to look over them."

"No. Not tonight. I just want a bed and about ten hours of sleep." He settled in the seat next to Silas and dropped his head back to rest on the leather.

"The bed I can do, but the sleep will have to be cut short. We need to leave for Avery by ten."

Trey flipped his wrist up and glared at his watch. "What the hell, Si, it's already three in the damn morning."

"I told you to sleep on the plane." When Trey growled, Silas grinned. "Look, you don't have to be at the school until two. You can sleep on the drive over; it's like what, two, three hours. The check presentation will last maybe an hour. We do a few interviews, a few photo ops, and then you can crash somewhere for a few hours before the game."

"What game?"

"The high school game. It's Homecoming. When I called about the check presentation they went nuts. They want you to crown the queen."

"No." Trey didn't' want any part of the celebration.

"Think about what it could do for your future."

He couldn't. All he could feel was his past. Senior Year. Homecoming King. He'd had no choice but to take Sunny Debona to the Homecoming Dance in the gym. Jordan had refused to attend. He didn't want to watch Trey dancing with someone else all night. Trey didn't blame him especially when Sunny kissed him in the middle of the gym floor in front of everyone.

Trey ground his teeth together. "Why can't we just present the check and skip out. No need to suit and tie it after the check's delivered. That's the whole point of this publicity nightmare. Right?"

"Technically, yes. That's the feel-good moment, the giving back. The game and the reunion are for your fans. They like to see where their heroes come from, hear about their escapades in high school."

Trey stiffened. "That wasn't part of the deal."

"Get a grip, big guy. I hired this film crew. Nothing's going out that I don't approve first." He paused. "There's not something you need to tell me is there?"

"No." Trey shook his head. No one knew about him and Jordan so no one could spill his secret. If Jordan intended to capitalize on their past, he would have done it already. Hell, maybe Jordan had moved out of Avery and wouldn't even be at the reunion. He could be losing his shit for no reason.

"Good." Silas slapped a hand against Trey's thigh. "Now stop bellyaching. This is supposed to be fun."

Chapter Four
~ * ~ * ~

"All students and faculty, please report to the gymnasium."

Jordan stopped mid-sentence as the announcement came over the PA system. His gaze skipped over the class. All eyes were on him. Some held fear, while others reflected the typical teenage disinterest.

"What's going on Mr. Brooks?"

"I don't know, but everyone grab your books and line up."

"Are we in danger?" A thin panicky voice came from the back.

"No, they would have told us to lockdown if there was any danger." Jordan glanced toward the windows. A news van for Channel Five pulled into the parking lot. He wasn't the only one to notice it, or the police car already parked at the curb.

"We had the pep rally last night at the bonfire."

"I bet someone brought weed to school."

"Maybe it's a bomb threat."

"I hope not, the last one took hours and I have to be at work at three-thirty."

"Class!" They all quieted and looked at him. "We'll find out when we get to the gym. Until then, stay together and keep quiet in the halls."

He opened the door and stepped out into the already streaming mass of teenagers. His students, mostly seniors, followed him the length of the hall and down another hall before entering the gym. He stood along the wall with the other teachers while the students swarmed into the bleachers to find friends and take a seat.

"What's going on?"

Lydia Danvers, the tenth grade World History teacher, bobbed a shoulder up and down. "No idea. There weren't any assemblies scheduled for today."

"Yeah, I know. I saw a news van pull up right before we left the classroom. Maybe someone won an award or something. Wasn't the band up for band of the week?"

"More likely, one of them stole something." The other teacher's permanent frown deepened.

Jordan sighed and turned his attention back to watching the students. He didn't understand teachers like Ms. Danvers. If she didn't like the students, then why teach? The kids felt her animosity and responded in kind. He hoped he never reached her level of disillusionment.

While they waited for the rest of the student body to file in and find seats, the television crew hustled through the door and hurried to a cleared area in the middle of the bleachers. Jordan noted with some surprise there was already another film crew set up. A blonde guy in a business suit stopped his conversation with Jim Boutwell, the principal, to greet the new arrivals.

"Students, settle down, please."

Vice-principal, Tessa Garard stood on the stage at the front end of the gym with microphone in hand. "Everyone make room." She waited a few seconds for the stragglers to squeeze into a seat. "Good afternoon, students and faculty. I hope you all are ready for the Homecoming game tonight. We're all excited to find out who won the Homecoming Queen crown, but that's not why we're gathered. We have a huge Homecoming surprise for all of you." A few cheers rang out but were quickly silenced by the shushing of embarrassed friends.

"Before I make the announcement, we need to make sure our visitors are ready. Mr. Barton?"

The suited gentleman held up a hand in the classic "wait" gesture as he checked with the camera guys. In his pocket, Jordan's phone vibrated. Fishing it out, he saw Janice's name and number on the screen. She was working the day shift at the diner. Had something happened?

Turning his back to the crowded gym, he pressed the phone to his ear just as Ms. Garard started talking again on stage.

"Janice? Is everything okay? Did something happen to dad?"

"He's fine. Where are you?"

"What? I'm at school, you dork. You know we don't dismiss until three fifteen."

"What are you doing? Are you at your desk?"

Behind him, the vice principal's voice gained excitement. He pressed his free hand over his ear. "No, I'm at an assembly. Somebody's getting an award or something. What the hel…heck?" He auto-corrected in case anyone was close by. "Why are you acting more nutty than usual?"

"Because I know what's going on. Jordan, you need to prepare yourself…"

"…welcome home, Trey Bright!"

The phone nearly slipped free of his nerveless fingers. He twisted around so fast his elbow banged against the cement block wall. The pain was minor compared to the vise squeezing his chest.

Trey's six foot-two inch frame filled the doorway of the boy's locker room the same way he always had. He was only missing the black and red letterman jacket emblazoned with a cowboy, their school mascot. With easy grace, Trey lifted a hand and waved at the wildly screaming crowd of teenagers. The fifty-megawatt smile Jordan remembered flashed into existence. Jordan's knee went rubbery. Twenty long years and Trey hadn't changed much.

J.T. Cheyanne

Dark mahogany colored hair, trimmed neatly shined beneath the gym lights. High cheekbones, straight nose, full lips curved in a smile, strong square chin with a slight indentation. He couldn't see from the distance, but Jordan knew the eyes were brilliant blue beneath thick lashes every girl in Avery had envied. His muscled stature had only increased in size with maturity. The loose fitting black track pants and crimson t-shirt only emphasized the broad shoulders, thick chest and trim waist. There was no doubt, he was still devastatingly handsome.

"Jordan!"

Janice's voice in his ear dragged him out of the past.

"It's him." Lame as hell, but it was all he could think to say.

Janice groaned. "Damn, I was hoping to spare you that. He's here to present a check to the school."

Jordan nodded and then remembered she wasn't standing beside him. "They're doing that now. There's a film crew and everything."

"Of course there is. He's a household name. It's great publicity for him and his team. I heard they are going to do interviews with a few current students and faculty."

Jordan worked to swallow the swiftly beating organ suddenly filling his throat. Sweat broke out all over his body. His thoughts scrambled as air vacated his lungs. "I have to go. I need to…go…somewhere. I can't…"

"Calm down, Jordan. Breathe. The bell will ring in about two minutes and then you can hide in the bathroom or whatever." Janice paused. "Although, I think it would be better if you actually talk to him."

"No." His denial was swift and certain. The last thing he needed, or Trey needed, was for them to talk.

"Jordan?"

"What's up, Cowboys! Can I get a yee-haw!" The answering screams were deafening in the crowded gym. Trey's eyes swept the bleachers. Rooted to the spot, Jordan absorbed every blink, every smile and nod.

"I brought a little surprise for all of you." A large covered easel was brought out. Trey reached for the end closest to him and tugged. The veil slipped away to reveal a check. Jordan's eyes widened. One million dollars. Faculty and students cheered. Trey waited for them to quiet down again.

"I want to be clear. It's not just for athletics. Sports are important, but so are the arts and scholastics. For every football player or cheerleader with a dream, there's an artist or a math genius who also has a dream."

Jordan swallowed hard. Surely, Trey wasn't referring to him.

J.T. Cheyanne

"Jordan, did he just reference a math geek? 'Cause that's totally a reference to you."

Jordan couldn't answer even if he wanted to. Of all of the things he could have said; all the subjects he could have chosen, why had he gone with math genius?

Trey continued his little speech. "I hope that the staff here will use this money wisely. Buy books, buy sheet music, instruments, microscopes, and computers. Leave the building repair and parking lot to the county. Invest in the students. They are the future."

"Jordan!"

He was literally saved by the bell. Students spilled out of the bleachers, some intent on going home while most of them fast-tracked it to surround Trey. Teachers rushed to bring calm to the madness. Jordan hung up with Janice yelling his name and ducked out of the gym. Thank God, he didn't have bus duty and could escape to his classroom.

Hurrying along the hallway, he was bombarded by memories he usually managed to keep at bay. Memories of Trey and a teenage crush that had grown into so much more. There were so many days he walked the halls of Avery High School and remembered Trey there. Captain of the football team, Mr. AHS, the most popular guy in school, always with a smile for everyone.

And now, he was at the school again. The small town quarterback returned, a hero and role model to millions of people across the country. Those same millions of people who didn't know him, not the real Trey. Not like Jordan knew him. Because when he left Avery, he'd left all of that behind. He hadn't come out and he hadn't come back. Not once.

Jordan shoved into his classroom but restrained the urge to slam the door behind him. He didn't blame Trey for staying in the closet. It would have tanked his football career just like the guy who'd recently entered the draft as out and gay. That man sat on the sidelines on the weekends instead of playing a game he loved. No, Trey had made the right decision. As much as it hurt, Jordan understood.

To be fair, he couldn't blame Trey for not coming back either. It had always been their plan, to escape Avery and live in the city where restaurants stayed open after ten at night, where there were concerts, theatre and museums and…life. Trey had found that.

Jordan eased into the chair at his desk, dropped his head in his hands and closed his eyes. Twenty years fell away like shattering glass. The first day of summer break before their senior year, he'd been behind his parents' diner tossing garbage bags into the dumpster. A car full of the popular crowd pulled up on the side, just far enough down they could see him. Phillip McDaniel and Sybil Parker got out of the front seats. He'd started tossing bags faster, hoping to escape their attention.

"Jor-Danaaaaa." Even the echo of the nickname crawled down Jordan's spine. Although he'd never come out and told anyone he was gay, they had known. Phillip and Sybil had taunted him mercilessly. That day, Phillip had decided to toss him into the dumpster with the trash while Sybil stood by snapping pictures on her brand new cell phone.

They had struggled with Phillips smirking and shoving at him. He remembered his cheek striking the edge of the dumpster. There had been blood, a lot of it. Phillip had laughed and come after him again. Slender and wiry, Jordan hadn't been a match for the defensive lineman. There was no way to avoid the inevitable dumpster dive. No one, certainly not Jordan, had expected Trey to interfere, or stop Phillip. The teammates had come to blows. The girls' screams brought Jordan's dad outside. By the time it was all over, Jordan had wished to be anywhere else, even in the dumpster.

To Jordan's surprise, Trey had come by the diner the next day to see if he was okay. Trey sported a black eye and a split lip that cracked open when he'd smiled down at Jordan. Jordan had been both horrified and fascinated. He'd had a crush on Trey since middle school. He kept every clipping from the local paper and the school newspaper. He'd pilfered photos out of the yearbook stash since ninth grade.

With the guy of his dreams standing in front of him, he'd almost forgotten his own name, but somehow he'd offered an ice pack and free milkshake. To his secret delight, Trey had accepted. The summer and senior year that followed had been the most perfect time of Jordan's life.

The door to his classroom banged open. Jordan jerked to his feet, snatched from his memories.

"Sorry, I forgot my purse." Sophia Shiver, a senior in his last class gave an apologetic smile. "You okay, Mr. Brooks?"

"Yeah. I just…I'm tired. It's been a long week."

"How's your dad? Uncle Rob said he's still in rehab."

Jordan gave her a reassuring smile. "He's getting stronger. The stroke was moderate. He has some paralysis on his left side, but no obvious cognitive problems. Thanks for asking, and tell your uncle, I said hi."

"Will do, Mr. Brooks. He's going to be so jealous when I tell him Trey Bright was here, actually here in the gym. He tells me all the time he went to school with him. And you."

Jordan nodded. "He did; he was actually on the football team with Trey. He was Trey's favorite receiver if I remember right. He was pretty good with his hands."

"But, not so good with his grades. He says he wouldn't be stuck in Avery if he'd paid more attention in class. I am so out of here after graduation."

"You sound like Trey. He was always saying how much he wanted to get out of here."

Her eyes went as round as basketballs. "You guys were friends?"

More than friends. But, he couldn't tell her that. "That's so hard to believe? The jock and the math...teacher can't be best buds?" Geezus, he'd almost said genius. Would she catch the slip? Jordan forced a smile to curve his lips despite the dagger twisting in his chest.

"Trey was, he is, a great guy. We became friends after he begged me to help him get through Cal 2 our senior year. He was determined it wasn't going to drop his GPA."

"Wow. You should have stayed in the gym for the interviews. I bet Trey would remember you."

Oh, yeah. There was no doubt Trey would know exactly who he was.

"It was wicked cool talking to the reporter. I'm going to be on the evening news." She gasped and grabbed his arm. "You think the national news will pick it up?"

"I don't know. If his publicist has anything to do with it, I'm sure something will be aired."

She squealed as only a teenage girl could and then bounced up and down. Her fingers squeezed his forearm. "Ohhhhhh! You can talk to him at the reunion. Uncle Rob said he wasn't going, but I bet he changes his mind. He wasn't expecting Trey Bright to come back for it. I have to go so I can call him. Have a great weekend, Mr. Brooks."

When she darted out of the room, Jordan sank back into his chair. He hadn't expected to see Trey either. To his knowledge, Trey had never even glanced back at Avery, and he certainly hadn't visited, not even to see his parents. Trey spent his summers training and working out at the university. His parents went to visit him for the holidays and he'd moved them out of Avery the first year of his professional career. That had been Trey's plan as soon as the college offers started rolling into his mailbox.

There had been one exception by the time they graduated. Jordan was supposed to have gone with him.

Chapter Five
~ * ~ * ~

As the last of the students left the gym, Trey's smile dropped. Exhaustion returned with a vengeance. It wasn't just the after-effects of the game. The school, hell the entire town, haunted him. As soon as he'd crossed the town limits, he'd felt the old pressures, felt the weight of the expectations of the population. None of them knew him; yet, they all knew him. The superficial him. The athlete, the hometown son, the football standout, the pro-bowler, the endorsement king.

Trey rolled his shoulders to ease the tension. Silas hovered with the film crews so he took a moment to look around the gym. At some point, the walls had been painted. The bleachers were newish but worn. The state championship banners from his junior and senior years bracketed a banner bearing his name and old jersey number.

The roar of pep rallies rose from his memories, echoed by the squeak of sneakers from fast-paced basketball games. His gaze swung to the stage he'd crossed graduation night with such a feeling of freedom. He was finally leaving Avery behind. The future had been wide open before him. He'd had so many plans then, so much hope.

A face hovered at the edges of his memories. His eyes turned against his will to the corner nearest the exit. He almost expected to see him there, a skinny serious boy, bent over a book, shoving his glasses back onto his nose as his pencil flew rapidly over the paper in his lap. Invisible to the athletes and the fans around him, oblivious to same as he worked through whatever math problem consumed him. He was there at the gym, a place he hated, for one reason.

For Trey.

Ruthlessly, Trey shoved that boy back into the past. He refused to let the memories drag him down into the abyss. He twisted around searching for Silas. He needed to get the hell out of there. Thankfully, his agent was already striding toward him.

"Come on, I got us a room at the Holiday Inn, same place as the reunion. You can crash for a few hours while the staff tries to do something with that suit you stuffed into your duffel bag."

"We could always head home. They have their check."

"You know, all of this negativity, I'm starting to think you are trying to hide something. This place isn't nearly as bad as you tried to make me believe. They have a McDonald's for Christ sakes."

"Yeah well, you didn't grow up here with nothing to do on Saturday night except hang out in that parking lot. It's an hour drive to the nearest theater and curfews didn't mix well with the dinner and a movie date nights."

"I suppose. Still beats L.A. It seems like there's a cinema on every corner, and at least one of them stayed open around the clock. It was great if you had the money to get at ticket. If not, you were stuck on the streets. Mom wasn't so keen on the curfews. She just wanted me to stay out of sight while she entertained the latest john."

Trey's shoulders slumped. A broken heart versus a broken childhood. "Sorry, man. I'm being a shit. Let's go get ready for the game. High school ball is totally different than the professional games."

He dropped an arm around Silas's shoulders as they exited the gymnasium. The guy was pretty damned decent to be an agent. He'd heard all of the horror stories about agents stealing money or lowballing their clients, and who hadn't seen Jerry McGuire.

Something about Silas had been different than the other agents clamoring for his signature. Whatever had clicked in that first meeting had proven to be right. Silas had made both of them a lot of money in sixteen years with contract negotiations and endorsements.

Out in the bright sunshine, Trey squinted against the glare and braced for the rush. Instead, the schoolyard and parking lot were nearly empty. The few remaining students weren't even looking in their direction.

"Wow, talk about a humbling moment."

Silas glanced around and laughed. "I talked to the police chief on the drive over; he promised to clear everyone out. Looks like he's a man of his word."

"Davis Brady?"

"Junior."

Trey nodded. "Makes sense. He went to the Academy straight out of high school. Always wanted to be a cop just like his dad."

At the rented SUV, Trey claimed the front passenger seat. While the film crew loaded up the cameras, he checked his email and scrolled through his social media pages. He tucked the phone away when the back hatch slammed closed.

Reaching across his chest, he grabbed for the seat belt and missed. He twisted around in the seat and snagged the metal hook. Movement at the school doors caught his eye. A man dressed in khakis and a button-down shirt hurried toward the teacher parking lot. The gait was a bit off, but the way the man held his shoulders, slightly hunched as if expecting a blow, robbed his lungs of air.

It couldn't be.

Swift as the wind, a hand darted up and shoved glasses back up on the man's nose. Trey tried to muffle the gasp.

Jordan. It was Jordan.

Trey had witnessed that same unconscious gesture hundreds of times. He'd teased Jordan about it constantly on the afternoons they studied together. It had become a game between them. He'd silently count the quick jabs at the glasses. At twenty, he'd pull them free of Jordan's face, tap his lips and demand a kiss. They'd end up tussling over the glasses, arms and legs wrapped around each other, Jordan always on the bottom, flushed from exertion and breathing hard.

Trey's body responded to his memories, hardening and tightening in anticipation.

"Trey?"

A finger poked his shoulder. His head rotated on his neck by instinct. Silas's gazed at him with lifted brows.

"You see a ghost out there or something? You made a weird noise, and then I think you quit breathing."

Trey flicked a gaze at the backseat where the film guys were trying hard not to listen. "Nah, just twisted wrong. The ribs are still tender."

"Uh-huh."

The agent's attention swung to the window beyond Trey's shoulder and then back to his face. It was clear Silas didn't believe him. But, he didn't ask any questions. Putting the vehicle in drive, he headed out of the school parking lot.

Chapter Six
~ * ~ * ~

"Where are you? If you say home, I'm coming to get you." Jordan grimaced at the high pitch of Janice's voice.

"I think you're actually worse than my mother."

"Not funny, Jordan. Tell me where you are, and it better be within a mile of this place."

"Ah, yes. That's why you aren't married. You're bossy and demanding."

"I'm divorced because my ex liked to share his willy with other women. It had nothing to do with my attributes or lack thereof. I'm not letting you change the subject, or back out of this reunion. It is bad enough you chickened out of the ball game. I expect you to be here in the next ten minutes. You're supposed to be my date."

"Damn, I didn't get that memo. Was I supposed to match my tie to your dress?"

"Don't be a smartass, it doesn't suit you." He heard her sigh. "Look, Jordan. I know you're nervous about seeing you know who. But, honestly, I've been here for like thirty minutes, and he's not here. He left the game after half time. He's probably back on the jet to where ever he came from. I doubt he shows up at all, and if he does, it will be a quick bit for the cameras and then he'll be gone. You won't even have to see him."

Jordan lifted his head away from the steering wheel and inhaled deeply before exhaling slowly. "I'm in the parking lot. Give me a few and I'll come inside." He hung up and tucked the phone into his suit pocket.

As a lifelong resident of Avery and a teacher at the high school, there was really no way he could avoid the reunion. Bowing out of the football game had been easy. He rarely attended unless he had to sell tickets. But, the reunion was a completely different type of ball game.

It had been advertised over the radio and in the local paper. Signs were posted all around town, including the diner's bulletin board. Until the previous afternoon, he hadn't thought twice about attending the event. It was expected. It was something to do on Saturday night besides Netflix and chill. Not that he actually had anyone to Netflix and chill with at the moment.

Pushing the Dodge Charger's door open, he exited the car and turned to face the hotel. Had Trey gone back to New York? Or, would he show up for the reunion? Were they finally going to have a face to face? Probably safer to do it with a crowd anyway. No chance of anything personal.

J.T. Cheyanne

Jordan squared his shoulders and took the first step. Janice believed it was heartbreak that caused Jordan to dread the meeting. In a way, it was. But, it wasn't his own heartbreak. He'd been the one to fail Trey. Of all of his shortcomings, that was the one that bothered him the most. Maybe it was time to face the music. And maybe, he was stressing out for no reason.

~~*

"If this was a game, you wouldn't be arriving thirty minutes late," Silas grouched as the elevator descended to the lobby.

"I thought late entrances were fashionable at these things." Trey gave the other man a playful shove. "Besides, it'll give you better footage for whatever it is you intend to air. The room will be full of people instead of nearly empty." At least, he hoped it would be. He wasn't sure what his reaction would be when, or if, he saw Jordan. He hoped the crowd would distract Silas.

"That's true." Silas turned to Zack, the cameraman. "We'll hang back in the lobby and let him go ahead. Later, we'll need to get a shot of him and anyone from the football team. A group shot if possible. Damn it. I should have brought a football."

"I'm sure they'll have one there. Along with pom-poms, yearbooks, baseballs and the championship banner that was hanging in the gym. That's what they do for reunions isn't it?" As the floor indicator hit one, Trey took a fortifying breath. He had to keep his shit together in front of everyone.

"Couldn't tell you," Silas replied. "I didn't go to mine."

"What?!?" Trey yelled while Zack barked out a laugh. Trey spun around to stare at his friend. "You forced me into this circus, and you didn't go to your own?"

"I'm not the big shot quarterback like you are. Besides, I didn't graduate. Got my GED down at the Y and then did the junior college bit while I worked. No one from back in the day would remember me. I was a nobody."

"Don't downplay what you did, Si. You worked your ass off." Trey's shoulder bumped the smaller man. "And, I'll quit whining about being here. There's a bar if I remember right. I'll buy you three a beer."

"Better make it a six-pack," Zack offered. "I went to my ten-year reunion and the prom queen had five kids and a mouth like a truck driver; the former principal was in jail on drug charges and the captain of the football team was married and divorced three times and paying child support to all of them. I still thank God every night for my normal life."

"You call hanging out with professional athletes and movie stars normal?" Silas deadpanned.

"Well no, but you expect them to be a bit weird." Zack immediately flushed and started stuttering. "Not you…I didn't mean…"

"S'ok, I know quite a few strange ones just on my team alone." Trey smiled at the guy behind him in the elevator and stepped out.

"Watch out!"

Silas's shout was too late. He stumbled sideways as a smaller body crashed into him. Thin arms wrapped around his hips.

"OMG! I can't believe it's really you. My dad said he went to school with you, but I said nuh-huh, no way. I mean, how cool is that? My dad! My dad went to school with Trey Bright. The other kids told me I was lying when I told them. I begged him to bring me. He didn't want me to come, said I'd probably be disappointed. We got here a few hours ago and he told me to stay in the room 'cuz he wasn't sure if you'd be here, but then I saw you on the news at the high school here giving them some money. I was so excited I couldn't stay up there 'til he texted me so I've been sitting right here by the elevator hoping to see when you came down."

The boy, about twelve years old, stopped talking, took a deep breath and buried his head against Trey's stomach. He could feel the boy's entire body shaking with excitement. Waving off the hired security, he dropped a hand on the kid's shoulder. The youngster looked up at him with hero-worship in his eyes.

"What's your name?"

"Bryce Skipper."

"You're Matt's son?" Trey could see the resemblance. Matt had the same hazel eyes, slightly turned-up nose and sandy blond hair.

The boy's eyes went saucer wide. "You know my dad's name?"

"Sure, I do. We didn't just go to school together. Your dad was on the offensive line. He kept me safe on the field so I could make all of those passes."

"Wow," Bryce breathed. "For real?"

"Yup, he won a few awards. I bet he never told you that."

Bryce shook his head. "I didn't even know he played football."

Trey wasn't surprised. Matt had always been quiet by nature. He played football because his family expected it. Ice hockey too, in the colder months. But, it had been his father's passion, not his own.

"Spilling secrets, Trey? I thought you were the strong, silent type."

Trey looked up to see Bryce's father smiling at him. "Matt, hey man. Damn good to see you." The two men embraced briefly. "He looks just like you at that age."

"Dad, you didn't tell me you played football with him." Bryce released Trey and dove at his father. "He said you protected him and won awards for it. Do you still have them? Can I see them? I wanna put them in my room."

"Slow down, kid." Matt laughed. "We'll talk about that at home. You are supposed to be upstairs."

Bryce ducked his head. "I know. I just got excited."

"I think this is what he was after." Trey handed over a signed headshot courtesy of Silas's ever-present briefcase. Bryce took the photo and bounced toward the elevator.

"I'll see you later. I've got to get him back upstairs."

"Good to see you, Matt. He's a great kid."

As the elevator doors closed behind them, Silas clapped. "Perfect. Just the sort of thing I was hoping to get. You're always great with the kiddos."

"Because they are pretty straightforward. They tell you what they think without filter or ulterior motives."

"Was that true about his dad?"

"The awards? Absolutely. The kid wants a role model, he has the perfect one living in the house with him. Matt's always been a stand-up guy." Trey frowned at the camera, suddenly uncomfortable. What if Jordan was in there? "Are you going to film every conversation I have tonight?"

"Maybe."

Trey smothered a groan. He would have to trust Silas's discretion. "Maybe they have the hard stuff. I don't think beer's going to cut it."

Zack laughed. "Told you, my man."

They made it across the lobby to the entrance to the ballroom without running into more fans. Trey made eye contact with one of the two former classmates manning the sign-in table and got waved on inside. He stepped into a throwback to their senior prom.

Chapter Seven
~ * ~ * ~

Jordan looked up when a hush swept through the room. His eyes were immediately drawn to the door. Flanked by the suited guy from the school assembly and a cameraman, Trey stood like a returning king in the doorway. The wicked smile Jordan remembered far too well curved lush lips and made Trey's blue eyes sparkle. A black suit emphasized a powerful, toned body. Twenty years later, he was still Jordan's walking wet dream.

Applause snapped Jordan out of his stupor. Their classmates cheered and clapped for the hometown boy made good before several rushed forward to greet him. In seconds, Trey stood surrounded by a rapt audience of former classmates and teammates.

"You going to say hello?"

Jordan sighed. "Janice, please don't start. Again."

"What?" She gave him a big innocent eyed look before circling around him to stare at Trey and his fan club. "I remember the first time I saw you two together," she mused.

"Shush, woman. No one knows about that."

"Pish, no one is listening to us." She slid into the seat beside him, swirled her drink around in her glass, and much to his dismay, continued her reflection. "You'd blown me off. We were supposed to go into the city and see the new X-Men movie and get a decent meal. Maybe go early enough to do some shopping. I'd been looking forward to it all summer. I saved every penny I earned at the diner."

"I forgot you worked there that summer."

She snorted. "You had one thing on your mind. Him." She pointed across the room at Trey. "I couldn't believe it when I saw you through the windows sitting at your kitchen table. Studying when we were supposed to be living it up in the city. And then, he walked in. I remember grinning like a fool. I knew you had a huge crush on him. I think I literally fell out on your lawn when he pulled your glasses off and leaned in and kissed you."

Jordan couldn't stop the sad, reminiscent smile. "Yeah, he did that, a lot. Teased me all the time about my habit of shoving them up on my nose. I should have told you the truth about us. It was hard not to."

"Nah, I told you a million times. I get it. This town would have flipped on its collective ear if you two had come out. Trey wouldn't be where he is now that's for sure."

Slipping a hand around his bicep, she pressed her cheek against the other side. "You two were so in love. I could tell even then. I spent a lot of our senior year watching you two watch each other. Good thing teenagers are so self-absorbed. No one ever even suspected."

"And, it needs to stay that way. That's why I'm staying right here. There's no reason either one of us should have to re-visit the past. I'm sure he's moved on like I have."

Janice laughed loud enough to draw a few stares. Jordan dropped his eyes to the table in front of them to avoid the looks.

"Moved on? You? Since when?"

"I've dated," he said unable to hide the defensiveness. "And, there was Mike."

"Yeah, let's call ol' Mike up and ask him about that moving on. Poor guy never stood a chance. I tried to tell him not to when he told me he was going to propose. He got mad. Wouldn't listen. And, we know how that turned out."

Jordan was glad the shadowed corner hid the flush that heated his skin. "Marriage is a big step. I wasn't ready."

"And, you never will be because it won't be him."

Jordan's gaze lifted and zeroed in on Trey, standing in the center of the room still surrounded by admirers. The blond guy in the suit stood at his side while the cameraman caught everything on film. Was the blond Trey's date? Surely not. There hadn't been anything on the news about him coming out. Or, was that the point of his return and the camera? To step out of the closet.

"Who's that guy with him? You ever seen him before?"

Jordan wasn't surprised Janice's question mirrored his own thoughts. They knew each other better than siblings. He shook his head in response.

"You think it's his date?"

Jordan chuckled. "Get out of my head."

"No." Janice laughed. "I like it in there."

"Maybe, he's a reporter?"

"He doesn't have a mic or a notepad. A teammate?"

"How would I know?"

"You don't know his teammates?"

Jordan gave her a raised eyebrow look. "I didn't watch him play when he was right here in front of me. You think I watch on TV?"

"But, you went to all of the games. Football, basketball and baseball."

"He expected me to be there."

"Of course, he did. That's where his boyfriend was supposed to be."

"Don't call me that."

"It's what you were." Janice plunked her drink down on the table. "You hid what you felt to protect him. You aren't hiding anymore. He shouldn't be either."

Jordan placed two fingers against her lips. "How much have you had to drink?"

She held up three fingers.

"You can't out someone, Jannie. It's their decision. If that cameraman hears you, it could ruin his career."

Knocking his hand away, she pointed up at him. "Maybe then, you'd actually talk to him and tell him what happened."

Jordan's spine stiffened. "No. I wouldn't."

"You're too damn stubborn, Jordan Brooks."

~ * ~ * ~

Two hours into the reunion, Trey sat at a table in the middle of the ballroom. He'd circulated around the room right after his arrival, signing autographs, taking pictures, making small talk. But, for the last hour, he'd been swapping stories with his teammates. Several members of his high school football team, including Matt, reminisced about the two championship seasons. At his right, Silas asked questions while Zack circled the table and filmed everything. He responded when asked a direct question, smiled and laughed when expected. But, as he had all night, he scanned the room looking for Jordan.

Once or twice, he thought he'd spotted the other man, but hadn't been able to escape Silas's watchful eyes to find out for certain. The glimpses were driving him crazy. Was the man there, or not? He thought about asking outright, but that would be too obvious.

Movement at the bar drew his attention. He turned his head to see Janice Meeks glaring at him. He straightened in his seat. He remembered her. Jordan's best friend. But, why was she glaring at him? Had Jordan told her about them? When she broke eye contact and headed for the lobby, Trey surged to his feet. Conversation at the table ceased.

"Sorry, I have to go to the little boy's room." Silas started to rise. "No, you stay here. You might get a sneaky story out of them while I'm gone." He forced a grin when the other men loudly denied they would spill any tasty beans.

"Remember the pact. Homecoming pranks are blood sealed." He pointed at Matt. "Make them behave."

"Blood sealed? What's he talking about?" Trey heard Silas ask as he strode toward the exit.

Out in the hallway, he looked left and right, but Janice had disappeared. He checked for signs directing guests to the bathrooms, but no luck. How had she disappeared so fast? On a guess, he went left toward the lobby. He did a slow walk around and again came up empty.

"He's in the ballroom, a table in the back, but he's planning on leaving soon. It's hard on him to be in the same room as you."

Trey swung around. Janice stood a few feet away. Accusation colored her fiercely whispered words and anger marred her pretty features.

Hard for Jordan? That was bullshit. Trey closed the shallow distance between them, fighting to keep his own voice low. "I hear guilt can be a pretty harsh bedfellow. Cowardice even more so."

J.T. Cheyanne

The dull flush of her anger deepened. "Cowardice?" She poked a finger into his chest.

"You don't know a damn thing about him if you think he's a coward. You, Bright, are the coward. You always were. He was proud of you, proud to love you, but you hid him away. You kept him in the closet and took him out when you felt like it. And then, you were gone. Now, you call him a coward? That's priceless."

With a final look of disgust, she twisted around to head back to the reunion. Trey caught her arm and pulled her into an empty room. When the door closed, she shook free of his hold but didn't try to leave. Her face clearly showed her contempt.

"He knew I was leaving. He was supposed to meet me at the university. He never showed up." His tone defensive, he stared her down. Or, tried to. She glared right at back at him.

"And, you never thought to ask him why?" Something shifted in her eyes. Pain, if he read it correctly. "Of course you didn't. You're Trey Bright after all. You were all up in your new school, training and practicing with your new team. You didn't have time for a little boyfriend from back home. How long did it take you to realize he wasn't there?"

"I tried to call. No one ever told me a damn thing except he went on some vacation. He never returned a single message. I'm not the bad guy here."

She shook her head. "That's all the effort he was worth? A few telephone calls? Maybe, he was right all along. Just leave him alone, Trey. Go back to wherever you call home and live your lie of a life. He's made a life here, and he deserves more than playing second fiddle to your glorified career." He didn't try to stop her when she yanked the door open and stalked out.

Thoughts twisting and turning in his head, he slipped out of the room and sought out the bathroom. How long she'd asked. Trey knew the very day, down to the exact hour when Jordan should have arrived at his dorm. He'd been in the weight room, mandatory team workouts, but he'd known.

He hadn't even showered after the long workout. Instead, he'd raced back to his dorm, only to find it empty. His phone calls had gone unanswered, straight to voicemail. After tossing and turning all night, he'd tried to call the next morning before classes started. He'd called between classes and on the way to practice. He'd called every day for a week, even calling the diner and the house number when he'd become desperate.

He became so despondent his coach had called him in after practice. The man had not wanted to hear tales of a broken heart and that was without Trey telling him the love of his life was another man. Coach Payne had told him to suck it up and look forward instead of backward. High school crushes ruined dreams, or so Payne had declared. There was a bigger world out there, and Trey needed to walk into it.

And, he had, but had that been the best choice? He'd thought so until he'd come back to Avery for the damn reunion. Matt was married to his high school sweetheart, Maisey Buchanan, and they had three children with Bryce being the youngest. He wasn't the only one. At least three of his former teammates had twenty-year marriages on record. They had children, homes and lives like his parents and their parents had before them.

Trey thought about his penthouse in Chicago and the cabin outside of Aspen. He had the structures to make a home, but they were empty of anything except possessions.

A stray thought made him queasy. Janice said Jordan had made a life in Avery. Did that mean a married life? He had thought himself numb to the pain Jordan could inflict, but he found that wasn't true. Feeling sick, he flushed the toilet for effect and exited the stall intent on returning to the reunion and telling Silas he was heading up to bed.

In his haste to escape his thoughts, he didn't notice the other man standing at the sink until he ran headlong into him. The cacophony in his head ground to a halt when he looked into eyes as familiar as his own, eyes not covered by the thick lenses of glasses. His heart banged against his ribcage as if desperate to escape and surround the man staring at him with apprehension in his honey brown eyes.

~*~*~

Jordan stared at Trey. He couldn't move; his voice deserted him. A tingling sensation washed through his body from every point where they had collided. He wanted to run willy-nilly for the exit, and at the same time, he longed to step forward and embrace the man despite the glaring eyes filled with a pain he understood all too well.

He should have known Janice was up to something when she sent him to the lobby to look for her purse. She probably hadn't even brought a damn purse. She'd seen Trey out there and decided Jordan needed a little push.

"Umm, hey." Rusty and breathless. Jordan cleared his throat. "I, uh, that is…we…didn't think that you would, umm, that you'd come back. For the reunion." How lame could he be? Jordan wanted to close his eyes and disappear.

"It was a last-minute decision." Trey's gaze wandered over him. Jordan felt exposed and vulnerable, unable to hide in the deserted bathroom.

J.T. Cheyanne

"Tell me something," Trey said. "Would you be here if you'd known I was attending?"

The question pierced him like a knife in the gut. There was no way to miss the hidden meaning behind the words. But, the question was moot, wasn't it? He had known there was a possibility Trey would be there.

"Yes."

Trey shot him a disbelieving look.

"I saw you on the news, the check you gave the high school." Partially true. He knew it had been on the news, but he hadn't been able to watch. He had still been recovering from the shock of seeing Trey at the high school.

"You still live in Avery?"

Jordan nodded.

"It hasn't changed much."

"No." Jordan shrugged a shoulder. "Few more houses, a Dollar General store, a new gas station."

Trey took a step toward him. Jordan swallowed hard and held his ground.

"Why?"

One word, shaking voice, a wealth of meaning. And yeah, that was pain in those beautiful ice blue eyes. Jordan dropped his gaze to the floor. He'd thought about this moment for years; practiced the words, but faced with the reality of the man, he couldn't remember a single thing except how much it hurt to let him go.

"Trey, I…" He broke off when the door swung open. Suited guy gave them the back and forth before walking to Trey's side.

"Hey, man. I got worried. You've been gone for a bit. Thought maybe another kid had waylaid you." The man stuck his hand out. "I'm Silas Barton. I came with Trey."

Good manners required he accept the handshake. "Jordan Brooks."

"You here for the reunion?"

"I am."

"We're doing interviews with old classmates…"

"No," Jordan interrupted. "I'm sure his teammates have given you plenty of anecdotes. I was just a nerdy kid who loved math. We definitely didn't run in the same circles. Good luck with your season, Trey."

Jordan slipped around them and swung the door open. "Nice seeing you again, Jordan." He glanced back to see Trey had put himself between Jordan and Silas. He extended his hand. Reluctantly, Jordan grasped his hand and felt the hard square of a keycard against his palm. Somehow, he managed to keep his face neutral.

"Good to see you, too." Lie. It hurt. So deeply. He tried to pull his hand away, but Trey tightened his grip.

"Hey, you're good with numbers. Do you remember Carl's junior year jersey number?"

It was a trick question. Carl Mathers had worn the same number all four years of high school. He and Trey had arranged times to meet using their own code throughout that last year of high school. The "you're good with numbers" always preceded the time. Except this time, Jordan knew it wasn't a time, but a room number. And junior year, third year.

"Twenty-four," Jordan blurted.

Room three twenty-four, and Trey expected him to show up. Trey released his hand and mock punched him the shoulder. The smile did not reach the cold blue eyes. "That's right! Guess I owe Steve that beer after all."

Tucking his hand in his pocket to hide the keycard, Jordan nodded. "Glad to help. Take care, Trey." He didn't even acknowledge the other man standing at Trey's back.

In the hall, he rushed back to the ballroom. Janice materialized out of the crowd, face full of expectation. He wanted to throttle her. Turning away from her, he found their table and grabbed his suit jacket.

"What happened? Where are you going?"

With the key burning a hole in his pocket and his mind battling to contain painful memories, he only wanted to escape. He dodged past her reaching arms and hustled through the lobby. He didn't take a full breath until he was inside his car. Half a minute later, the passenger door opened. Janice fell into the seat and slammed the door.

"Jordan?"

He pulled the small square of plastic out of his pocket and tossed it across the seat into her lap. "He wants me to meet him in his room."

"Are you going?"

"No. Yes." Jordan banged a fist against the steering wheel. "I should. I owe him some kind of explanation."

"Just tell him the truth."

"There's no point, Janice. It's all in the past. He brought a guy back with him."

"His agent."

"What?"

"The guy is his agent. Silas Barton." Janice waved her phone at him. "I was curious. I took a picture and put it in Google images. It popped right up." She gave him a swift smile. "I knew you'd jump to that conclusion so I checked."

"Oh."

"Oh is right. He hasn't come out. There's nothing anywhere on the internet even speculating that he's gay. And, he's not linked to any women either. He's been declared the most eligible bachelor in pro football several times."

"You've been busy."

"When someone breaks your best friend's heart, you become the best P.I. in the world."

Jordan sighed. "It was the other way around and you know it. I broke his heart. He didn't do anything wrong."

Janice sneered at him. "In twenty years, he couldn't come back here and check on you? That's bullshit. If he loved you like he said he did, he would've come back to see what the hell was going on."

"I'm glad he didn't."

Janice went still. "Why?"

"If he'd come back, he would have stayed. He would have lost his scholarship. He would have been miserable." Jordan reached over and picked up the keycard. He brushed a thumb over the Holiday Inn logo.

"All he ever wanted to do was get away from Avery. He knew being gay in such a small town would be hell on both of us. He was right. Football was the only way he was going to get out. I understood that, accepted it."

"But, you were so sad."

"Yeah. I knew there would never be another one like him. Not for me. I loved him so much I had to let him go. I thought I was over him, but seeing him here tonight was a solid punch in the gut."

Reaching over, she took his hand and squeezed. "Think about it hard. You may not get another chance."

"I know."

"Maybe, he just wants to see if the sex is as good as he remembers."

Jordan groaned.

Chapter Nine
~ * ~ * ~

After considerable grumbling on Silas's part and outright evasiveness on Trey's side, he finally stood in his hotel room. Alone. Shrugging out of his suit jacket, he tossed it across the lone chair in the room. The tie came off next and followed the same path.

He sat on the edge of the bed and fell back. Exhaustion clawed at him, but anticipation raged a fierce war to keep him awake. Closing his eyes, he tried to remember every detail of the brief encounter in the bathroom.

First impression, Jordan wasn't the skinny kid he'd been in high school. He'd definitely grown up. Jordan's dark suit had molded a trim, athletic frame that left Trey with an urgent need to explore. Thin and lanky arms and legs were rounded with muscle. His chest was thicker, waist slim. A man's body filled out perfectly.

The thin, angular face he remembered was fuller, the jawline firm and strong. A five o'clock shadow had darkened Jordan's cheeks, drawing attention to the pink fullness of his lips. The light brown hair was the same, but no longer fell into his eyes which meant he actually remembered to get a haircut. The glasses were gone, probably had contacts. The thought started an ache in Trey's chest.

Jordan had been nervous but hadn't been surprised to see Trey. He'd stood his ground when Trey invaded his personal space, something the teenage Jordan would have never done. Constantly bullied and ridiculed because of his small size and big glasses, Jordan had tried to avoid confrontations whenever possible.

Trey had never intervened. It wasn't until the day at the diner when the bullying touched something personal within him that he'd finally stepped up. He had quit denying his own sexuality a few years prior, but only to himself. He hadn't been willing to admit it to anyone in Avery. If they knew, he had no doubt he would have been in Jordan's shoes.

A soft knock brought him to his feet. Self-consciously, he ran a hand over his hair and stared at the door. His heart thrummed painfully in his chest. Sweat dampened his palms. He had thought he was prepared for the long-overdue showdown, but his body and his heart were telling him otherwise. Unsettled by his reaction, he stalked across the room and snatched the door open.

"I gave you a…"

"I'll only be a sec, forgot my charger."

Trey almost shouted with frustration and then disgust. Why was he getting himself so worked up?

Silas sailed past him into the room with his nose buried in his phone, but it didn't keep his attention. From the doorway, Trey watched the other man's eyes flick around the room.

"There's no one here, Si." Unfortunately. "You want to check the bathroom before you leave. Maybe grab the shampoo or soap?"

Silas held up the charger and grinned. "Nah, got what I need right here."

"I'm not opening the door again so you better be sure."

"Harsh, my brother."

"A kick in the ass is harsher still. Want to find out?"

Silas rolled his eyes and shrugged. "Just be careful, eh. With cellphones and social media, one thoughtless moment can haunt you for years."

"So taking out my agent would be career-ending?"

"In more ways than one, bub." Silas slipped between Trey and the door. Standing in the hallway, he looked left and right. "I don't see any cameras out here, but you never know. People make fast money selling secrets about stars and athletes."

"Geez, Silas, I know. I might have been raised in the back of nowhere, but momma didn't raise no fool." He shut the door as the man walked toward the elevator chuckling. He needed to face facts. Jordan wasn't going to show. Just like the last time.

~*~*~

Trey fought his way out of a deep sleep. Limbs shaky and weak refused to follow his commands. He blinked against the darkness. Something had registered on his subconscious mind. He reached for the lamp at the same time a moan full of terror sank into his foggy brain.

The light washed over Jordan, sitting in the lone chair which he'd pulled to the foot of the bed. The other man had leaned over to rest his head on the mattress and must have fallen asleep. He was dreaming, and from the twitches and groans; it wasn't pleasant.

Frozen to the spot, Trey could only stare at the oblivious man. At some point during the early hours of the morning, he'd shown up. Trey had given up when two a.m. rolled around. He'd taken a sleep aid and gone to bed. He hadn't been in the best place to handle Jordan's rejection a second time.

Except, Jordan was right in front of him.

Another groan, more intense, escaped Jordan. The hand resting against the bedspread clenched and unclenched. Trey sat up and reached for it, but stopped before actually making contact. While he hesitated, Jordan's entire body jerked as if electrified. A hiss of pain slipped through

J.T. Cheyanne

clenched teeth. Trey made up his mind. Sliding to the end of the bed, he grasped Jordan's shoulder and shook it.

"Jordan, you're dreaming. You need to wake up." When there was no reaction, he shook harder. "Jordie! Wake up!"

With a quick lurch, Jordan sat up. Eyes still dazed by sleep met his own.

"Trey?"

"Jordan."

Jordan's head swiveled as he looked around the room. It took a few moments for things to register, and then his gaze swung back to Trey.

"You were asleep when I came in; you looked pretty wiped out."

"I took some melatonin. I didn't think you were going to show up." Trey hesitated. "Again."

To his credit, Jordan flushed and dropped his eyes to his lap. "I almost didn't." He shifted a few times before he finally spoke again.

"You'd think after twenty years, I'd know what to say to you. I've had this conversation a thousand times in my mind."

"Don't bother with lies, and I don't want your excuses. I want the truth."

Jordan flinched away from the harsh words. He swallowed once. Nodded. "I understand."

"No, you don't." Trey surged to his feet and paced away from the bed. "I left here thinking you were going to meet me. I counted every day we were apart. The day you were supposed to get there, I couldn't concentrate in the gym. I was just that excited. And then, you didn't show up. You didn't call. You wouldn't answer my calls."

"I'm sorry."

"You're sorry?" Trey scoffed. "You nearly broke me, Jordan. I almost lost my scholarship. I couldn't focus on anything except you not being there." His fury and pain bounced around the room finding soft targets in the man hunched in the hotel chair. "Why, Jordan? Why didn't you come?"

"I couldn't."

"Bullshit." No way was he buying that.

"It's the truth, Trey, whether you believe it or not." Jordan's voice dropped even lower. "You weren't the only one who suffered. I loved you, Trey. You were everything good in my life. I wanted to be with you more than you'll ever know."

"I don't believe you." Trey stalked back around the chair, waiting until Jordan lifted his head and their eyes collided. Jordan wore a defeated look. Trey had seen it before. It launched him right back to that spot behind the diner. The taunts and insults from Sybil and Phillip. It wasn't the only time he'd seen that expression, but it had never been because of him. It nearly cooled the anger. Nearly.

"You know why I don't believe you?" When Jordan didn't respond, Trey continued. "I called back here every day. Your house, my house, the diner. At first, no one answered the damn phone. And then, no one knew where you were because you and your parents went on a surprise vacation. I left messages on your phone and on the house phone. You never returned any of them. You threw everything we had away and you didn't even have the balls to tell me why."

Bitterness tasted foul in his mouth. Trey twisted away and yanked open the mini-fridge. He cracked a bottle of water and took a long swallow. While he did, Jordan rose from the chair and picked up his jacket. He looked at Trey with sad eyes.

"Hurting you will always be the biggest regret of my life. I wish...,"

Jordan's voice broke. He raised a hand to wipe away the tear spilling down his cheek. Trey refused to acknowledge the evident pain shimmering around Jordan. He couldn't allow himself to give in, not even a fraction or he'd be lost.

"It doesn't matter what I wish. I had to make a hard choice. I did what I thought was best for you."

"What choice?" Trey bit the words out through clenched teeth. "We discussed everything before I left. Your parents, your education. My scholarship. My parents. The dorm. Everything. All of the choices were hashed out over and over again."

Jordan shook his head. "Not all of them. We were so naïve."

"Damn it, Jordan. I have a right to know whatever it is you're hiding. Your so-called choice affected my life, too."

"Rise and shiiii…umm…hello again." Silas's head did a quick swivel, easily reading the tension in the room. He pasted on his agent smile. "Jordan, isn't it?"

Jordan ignored the outstretched hand, but he nodded. Trey wanted to throttle Silas.

"You forget how to knock?"

Silas shrugged and held up a keycard. "You didn't answer the text messages I sent. I thought you were still asleep."

"Obviously not. I'm busy." In truth, he'd been so focused on Jordan, he hadn't heard the phone and had no idea what time it was.

"The jet is supposed to leave at ten. We need to get on the road if we're going to make it back."

Trey raked a hand over his hair. "Fine. But, I need a minute. Can you just get the hell out?" Not exactly polite, but Trey wasn't feeling so agreeable at the moment.

J.T. Cheyanne

"No," Jordan said. "I should go."

"We aren't finished talking." Trey didn't care what Silas thought. He knew he could trust the agent's discretion if and when needed. At the moment, he wanted answers, and Jordan hadn't given him any.

"We're just beating ourselves up, Trey."

Misery shadowed Jordan's face. Trey didn't want to see it. He didn't want to acknowledge Jordan's pain. He wanted, needed, something to ease the relentless ache that lived inside his chest, a persistent parasite that took up residence the day he'd flown out of Avery. He crossed the room and grabbed Jordan's arm. He pulled the other man off balance and into his body. He put his lips to Jordan's ear.

"If what we shared meant anything to you, you won't go out that door."

Trey stepped back. Jordan paled but nodded once. His eyes flicked to Silas.

Trey kept his eyes and his hand on Jordan. "Silas. I need you to leave."

"Trey, we really have…"

"Get. Out."

With a frustrated sigh, Silas opened the door. He looked back over his shoulder.

"Just go, Si." Trey was seriously worried he was going to punch the man if he didn't leave.

When the door finally clicked closed, he realized he couldn't move away from Jordan. His feet ignored the command to move. His hand refused to release Jordan's arm. Instead, he had the incredible urge to move closer, to align their bodies and see how they fit together. Jordan was taller, his body a man's body instead of a teenager's lanky arms and legs. The curve of his jaw bore the shadow of a beard, something he'd never had in high school.

Chapter Ten
~ * ~ * ~

He couldn't breathe, couldn't think. Trey was too close. The vise of Trey's grip around his forearm scalded the skin beneath the cotton sleeve. The hot sweep of Trey's breath skipped across the nape of his neck. His feet felt like they were bolted to the floor. That changed when Trey's soft lips brushed over his cheekbone.

Knees rubbery, he would have fallen except Trey's arm slid around his waist. Jordan sucked in a shuddering breath. Instead of moving away, Trey stepped closer. Jordan's heart slammed against his ribs. He needed to stop Trey. It had never occurred to him that the key card meant sex. It wouldn't make the problems go away; it would make them worse. He tried to pull away, but Trey moved with him.

"Trey, we can't do this." Not the hardest words he'd ever spoken, but damn close.

"Why not? You married?" Skilled lips found his earlobe and suckled. Jordan's entire body trembled.

Wait, what was the question? Married?

"Ah, no."

"Relationship?" Trey's nose rode up the shell of Jordan's ear. The hand at his hip slid down to squeeze his ass.

"No."

As if given an all-access pass, Trey shifted them until Jordan's back hit the wall. Trey crowded in close, palms on ass cheeks, and sweet fucking geezus, he claimed Jordan's mouth. The kiss burned through the scars and pain and heartache to fire the very center of his being.

He quit being kissed and responded. His hands roamed over the sculpted muscles in Trey's back, some familiar and some not. The taste and smell of Trey filled his senses. Memories crashed through ironclad barriers with hurricane strength. And with them, came the tentacles of anxiety that robbed him of breath. Panicked, he struggled against Trey's hold.

"Fuck!"

Jordan sagged against the wall, tried to focus on his breathing and watched Trey stalk away. Hands that weren't quite steady raked through his hair before Trey swiveled back to stare at Jordan.

"That shouldn't have happened."

It took massive effort, but Jordan pushed himself off the wall and stood up straight. He refused to wipe the wetness from his cheeks. He wanted Trey to see his pain, to understand he wasn't the only one who'd suffered.

J.T. Cheyanne

"You're right," he agreed. "I didn't come here for a hook-up." Trey's eyes went flat and hard. Jordan averted his eyes. "I should go. You're going to be late."

"The jet won't leave without me and Silas knows it. I'm not going anywhere until you tell me why, Jordan. Why did you rip us apart at the seams? Was it your parents? Did they stop you when you told them?"

It would be so easy to let them take the blame; they had even offered to be the scapegoats. But, he couldn't do that.

"No. Mom and Dad have always known I'm gay. They knew about us. They protected us while you were still here, telling church members and customers how hard you studied to be eligible for college ball. They were as proud of you as I was. Dad watches all of your games. He even has a jersey framed and hanging at the diner."

"So why skip town? Why the lies? Why didn't you answer my calls?"

"I wasn't on vacation, that much is true, but I also wasn't in Avery. I didn't get your messages until months later. Your season had started. Everyone was talking about the rookie quarterback with the impressive stats. You were meant for so much more than Avery, so I made the choice to cut the ties. It hurt like hell. More than…" Jordon bit his lip, still holding back the one piece of information Trey wanted.

"It was the best decision for you."

Trey stormed across the room and grabbed Jordan by the shoulders. Fury danced wicked flames in his eyes. "A decision I wasn't given a say in? How can you say it was best for me when I didn't even know a decision was being made? What the hell was going on, Jordan? We were supposed to be a couple, a team. If it was something here, I would have come back for you."

Jordan's already cracked and bleeding heart, shattered into tiny pieces. "I know you would have," he whispered. "That's why I couldn't tell you. Why I won't tell you."

Trey shoved him away. Jordan stumbled but caught himself before he fell. It tore him apart to see the jagged lines of pain on Trey's face. He wanted to comfort but knew he would be rebuffed. He wanted to tell Trey he still loved him; he'd never stopped. That's why he hadn't been able to marry Mike. The marriage would have been doomed before it ever started.

Instead, he picked up his jacket and folded it carefully over his arm. "You're living your best life, Trey. You have the career you always wanted. You're famous. You travel the world. If you'd come back to Avery, your life would have been interrupted. Millions of little boys wouldn't have a hero. And, you'd be stuck here. You would have hated that."

"You're wrong, Jordan. My best life included you. I'm living the alternative." Trey walked past him and went into the bathroom. "I should have never let Silas talk me into coming back here. You can let yourself out. See you in another twenty years. Maybe."

The soft click of the bathroom door closing sheared through Jordan like a shock wave. He lurched toward the exit door and fumbled with the knob before he could actually get it open. Out in the hall, it took him a moment to focus and start the long walk to the elevator.

Chapter Eleven
~ * ~ * ~

"What the hell do you mean, the jet has a mechanical problem? It's just been sitting there since we flew in on the damn thing."

"I know, but the pilot says some light came on during the pre-flight check so he's called in a mechanic. He's supposed to be at the airport this afternoon and will hopefully have it fixed quickly."

"I have to be in New York tonight. I have an interview that you set up." Trey resisted the urge to kick and throw things. It had taken him thirty minutes after Jordan left to stop the tremors shuddering through his body. He'd refused to allow the tears burning against his eyelids to fall.

The ache in his chest had only intensified. It throbbed with every breath. Nervous energy chased through his system. He couldn't sit still, he couldn't focus. Memories bombarded him.

"If it's a major issue, we can book a domestic flight."

"Why can't we do that now?" Trey didn't often make demands, not from his team or his agent. But, he desperately needed to get the hell out of Avery before he lost his shit. Silas was catching the brunt of his misery.

"Most of the stuff for the children's hospital is still on the jet. So, if we leave it here, I have to figure out a way to ship everything back to New York."

"I should have never let you drag me out here. I told you it was a bad idea." Trey dropped into the wingback leather chair in the hotel lobby.

"Seems to me, you were having a good time. Until this morning."

"Stop right there, Silas," he growled. "Jordan is off-limits."

"Fine. But, we have some time to kill while they figure out what's wrong with the jet. You want to head into town and get in a few more interviews."

"No. I absolutely do not want to see anybody. I want the jet fixed so we can leave."

Silas shrugged. "Fine, I've already checked you out, but I can rent another room for you. You can go back upstairs and catch up on your sleep."

"Why can't we just head to the airport and wait there?"

"You know how uncomfortable airports are." Trey got the distinct impression Silas was determined to stay in Avery. He would bet his next paycheck he knew why.

"They have hotels close to the airport. There's no reason to stay here."

"I told you I can work in a few more interviews, get in a few shots of the football field, the school, that sort of thing. Zack and I can make the rounds."

"You didn't get enough of that stuff at the assembly or the game Friday night?"

"The stadium will be empty today."

"Whatever." Trey pointed a finger at his agent. "But, you stay away from Jordan."

"Melodramatic much?" Silas rolled his eyes and chuckled.

"Silas." Trey rose to his feet. "Leave him alone."

"Fine. I promise I won't seek him out, but if Avery is as small as you continuously claim, I may run into him by accident."

Forty-five minutes after Silas left, Trey paced back and forth in a room identical to the one he'd checked out of earlier. He had tried to review film of the game, made a half-hearted attempt at studying the new plays, and had flipped through every channel on the television at least three times. Restless energy refused to let him settle. There was no hope of sleep.

Every time he closed his eyes, his entire being focused on Jordan. It was excruciating to know he was so close and yet so far away. Especially, when he still didn't have any answers. Whatever had happened, Jordan steadfastly refused to tell him.

The restless energy ramped up even as his body went stone still. Janice knew. And, she was as close as Jordan. In a matter of minutes, he was downstairs and out the door with Janice's address clutched in his hand.

~*~*~

"You should have just told him the truth. It can't change anything now."

Janice came out of his kitchen carrying the quart of Ben and Jerry's Cherry Garcia and two spoons. She fell into the couch beside him and propped both feet on the coffee table. He took the spoon she offered and avoided the questions in her eyes.

"Exactly. So, there's no need to re-hash the past."

"Re-hash implies there had been some hashing to start with, bubba. You're a teacher; you're supposed to know that."

"Math, woman. I teach math."

"And, you speak English. When you re-turn, you come back to the same spot. When you re-ignite, you light the same fire again."

"You're pushing it with that first one."

"But it makes my point."

He knew there was no winning the argument. Janice played in her own sandbox. The few people she allowed into that sandbox accepted she was different. But then, most of them were different as well.

Claire was deaf, so they'd all had to learn ASL. Billy had been born with Down syndrome. Janice was bipolar. From an early age, she'd had issues controlling her moods and her anger. Jordan hadn't had any health issues, but Janice had responded to and connected with him from the day she moved into Avery with her parents. The newest member of the little group was Carter Lee. He was everything Jordan had been in high school, the stereotypical nerd. And, if Jordan read him correctly, he was also gay. They hadn't actually discussed it.

He scooped out a large spoonful of the ice cream and shoved it in his mouth. Janice shook her spoon at him.

"What if you tell him the truth and he decides to come out? What if he gives it all up for you? You ever think of that?"

Jordan swallowed. "Alone at night in the dark, yeah, of course, I have."

"Well, that can't happen if he doesn't know."

"You just keep beating a dead horse. He's gone. His agent said the plane was leaving at ten and they had to drive to Jackson Hole." Jordan definitely didn't want to dwell on Trey's leaving again. He pushed up from the couch. "You're welcome to stay, but I need to go in and help mom at the diner. The breakfast crowd will be cleared out by the time I get there. You working today?"

"Yeah, but not until four. She wants me to help out with the game crowd."

"Lock up when you go. Love ya, mean it."

On the short drive into the middle of Avery, he tried to focus on what he needed to do when he got to the diner. But, after being relegated to a corner of Jordan's mind for too many years, Trey refused to stay in the gilded cage. His smile, his eyes, the deep timbre of his voice. That Kiss.

Jordan's fingers tightened around the steering wheel. He hadn't told Janice about That Kiss. She was already in a hypomanic state about Trey's visit to Avery. If she knew Trey had kissed him, she'd never let the subject drop.

With a will of its own, his mind re-played, haha Janice, That Kiss. Trey's hand wrapped around his bicep. The slightly larger, but still familiar body pressed along his side. The warmth of Trey's breath against his cheek and neck. That moment when their lips brushed ever so softly, and then the heated invasion of Trey's tongue.

A full-body shudder worked its way through Jordan. The strength and possessiveness he remembered had almost been his undoing. If Trey hadn't moved away, if he'd kissed him again, Jordan would have probably spilled every secret he had, even those not his own.

As he turned into the diner, he breathed a quick sigh of relief. The customers and his momma would keep him distracted. He pulled behind The Table Top and parked. Smoke curled into the air so someone had already started the grill. Just inside the back door, he found the culprit.

"Dad, it's good to see you out, but does Mom know you're here?" He leaned down to hug his father. The embrace was returned, but only with the good right arm.

"I rode over with her. I was going stir crazy in that house all by myself. Doc said I could just hang out back here. Nothing strenuous."

"I guess that means lighting the grill is okay?"

"Light a match, hit the gas, what's hard about that?" His dad tried to wink, but his facial muscles were still a bit weak.

"Nothing at all. Guess I better get the meat on so we don't disappoint our customers."

"I'll help."

"No, Dad. Those boxes venture into the strenuous side of the job. Momma would have both of our heads and you know it. I can do it."

While he carted boxes outside and loaded the big cooker, his dad moved his chair outside. Jordan smiled and shook his head as his father issued instructions. With the meat set, he retrieved another folding chair from the office and plunked down next to his dad. Their breath misted in the chilly air.

"So, I saw on the news that Trey was back in town."

Jordan groaned and let his head fall back. He stared up at the blue, nearly cloudless sky. He was so very lucky that his parents accepted him for who he was. He knew that, celebrated it and thanked the good Lord for it. But, right at that moment, he wished his dad didn't know. Trey was the last thing on Earth he wanted to talk about. However, he knew he couldn't pretend he hadn't heard.

"Yeah. Big check for the school and he was at the reunion last night." He tried hard for indifference, but his voice cracked and there was no way his dad missed it.

"I take it things didn't go well."

"He wanted answers, wanted to know why I didn't show up, why I didn't call."

"To be expected. You two were an item for over a year." His dad reached over and patted his hand. "I don't suppose you told him."

"No, dad. There's no point."

"Maybe, maybe not."

Jordan shot up out of his chair and paced over to the grill. "You sound like Janice. I left her at my house eating ice cream and parceling out advice that I should chase him down at Jackson Hole and spill my guts."

"Always was a smart girl."

Jordan wheeled around to stare at the older man. "Dad, seriously?"

His dad gave him a lopsided smile, the left side not moving too much. "Come and sit down, son. You don't want to talk about Trey, we won't. I just hate knowing you're hurting and don't say you aren't. I'm your dad. I can see it in your eyes and on your face. And, if I can see it, your mother will lock on like a fighter pilot."

Jordan paced back to the chair, sat, took a long inhale and let it out slowly. "He still takes my breath away. He's my Trey, and he's not. He kissed me." Jordan brought his fingers up to his lips, realized what he was doing and let his hand fall back into his lap.

"He was angry, furious actually. Not about the kiss. Before. He was angry before he kissed me. His agent interrupted us and I tried to leave. He grabbed me by the arm and pretty much demanded I stay. The guy left. I wasn't…I didn't expect it…it blew my mind."

His dad chuckled. "First loves can do that to you."

"But, it's been two decades, Dad, and still the spark was instantaneous."

"That's called a soul mate, son, and you're letting him go without putting up a fight."

"You think that's what I did the first time?"

"No." His dad reached over and patted his hand again. "That was entirely different. I know how hard that was for you. I was and am very proud of you for putting him first when you were in such terrible pain. You cried out for him so many times, it broke my heart. I almost gave in and called him several times."

Tears stood in his father's eyes. "Your mother and I were of little comfort. We tried, Janice tried, but you needed him. Especially later."

Jordan turned his hand over and clasped his dad's hand. "I would have been furious with you both. It would have ruined what he has now."

"Maybe he would have rather been with you. Maybe none of that matters as much to him as you think it does."

Jordan looked up at the sky, at the grill and finally back at his father. "He said that this morning, or pretty much."

"Oh?"

"I told him he was living his best life and he denied it, said I was his best life and he was living the alternative."

J.T. Cheyanne

"Oh, Jordan." Disappointment colored his father's words. "And you let him walk away after that?"

"Actually, he tossed me out of his hotel room." Jordan gained his feet and walked to the grill. He checked the meat he'd only just put on to cook and closed the lid again. Emotions tumbled through him like fall leaves. Hope, fear, love, uncertainty, anger, sadness, shame, guilt.

"I gave him up a long time ago. I made a life here without him. It's been hard as hell, but I've survived. I couldn't give him up again; I wouldn't survive that loss a second time."

"Who says you have to?"

Jordan turned around to look at his dad. The signs of the stroke were fading, but there were still obvious to him. He tried for a smile but knew it wasn't convincing. He also knew telling his dad everything was going to be okay wouldn't work either. Despite the stroke, his mind was still sharp.

"You know his contract is under negotiations right now. You saw what happened to that college kid that was openly gay. They ignored him in the draft. Trey can't afford to come out, it would tank his career."

"Doesn't he have the right to make that decision instead of having it made for him?"

The bottom fell out of Jordan's stomach. He spun around to find Trey standing at the edge of the diner. Trey spared him an unpleasant frown before pasting on a smile and walking over to greet Jordan's dad.

"Hey, Mr. B., how's it goin'?"

Jordan hurried to his dad's side and helped him up out of the chair. Trey embraced the older man and gave him a genuine smile, not the playboy smirk that melted hearts all over the U.S.

"All good, my boy, all good. Had a stroke a while back, but this old body is still kicking."

Trey shot a worried glance at Jordan.

"It was on the mild side, but there's been a bit of paralysis," he said to Trey. "Dad, why don't you sit back down?"

"No, no. I'll go inside, let the two of you talk." He took Trey's hand with his good one. "You come inside before you leave. You can sign the jersey I have hanging on the wall, get a picture to go with it."

"I sure will, Mr. B., be glad, to."

They waited in silence for Jordan's dad to make it inside.

"So, you're making decisions for me again?"

Jordan flushed. There wasn't much he could say in response so he said nothing. Instead, he waved at the chair his dad had just vacated.

"I'll get us a drink. You still a cherry Coke guy?"

"Just sit, okay. I didn't come for a drink or food."

"I thought you were already gone."

"Jet issues, or so Silas says. I'm not sure I believe him." Trey shrugged. "Truth or not, I'm stuck here until sometime this evening."

"So you came looking for me?" Jordan couldn't hide the surprise in his voice.

"No." Trey slid down in the chair and stretched his long legs out in front of him. Jordan's mouth went dry. He forced his eyes away from the display of masculine beauty spread out like a feast.

"I came back to pry some answers out of Janice." Jordan's gaze snapped back to Trey's face. "You needn't worry. The only thing she would tell me is that you were here. I don't think that she likes me very much."

"She's a bit protective."

"She's downright hostile, and I never did anything to her. Or to you."

Jordan closed his eyes and sent a silent prayer heavenward. "I know, and I've told her that so many times."

"She knows what happened after I left."

"She does, yes."

Trey shot up out of the chair. "Does everyone here know?"

"No, not everyone. I wasn't living in Avery."

Trey swung back around to glare at him. "Would you stop being so damned cryptic? Why is it so hard for you to just be honest with me? Don't you think I should hear it from you?" He stalked back across the small lot and bent over Jordan, caging him between his arms as he grabbed the arms of the chair.

"You weren't living here? Where the hell were you?"

Jordan pressed his lips together and stared at Trey.

"You aren't going to answer that are you?"

Jordan shook his head despite the spark of pain in Trey's eyes. Anger quickly snuffed it.

"Silas is in town, too. He's doing more interviews. He saw you in my hotel room this morning. Don't you think he'll be asking the good people of Avery why you were there or what went on between us?"

"Tutoring," Jordan replied. "That's all anyone here knows about us. They don't have secrets to tell. We made sure of that."

Jordan stared up at him and That Kiss rippled through his mind. Even angry, Trey was gorgeous. Fire sparked in those blue, blue eyes. Sensual lips pressed in a tight line, but Jordan knew they were soft and lush. He longed for the freedom to reach up and slide a palm around Trey's neck and pull him down for another kiss.

Something in his face must have given him away. Trey's eyes darkened, the pupils expanded. The harsh slash of his mouth eased and his

J.T. Cheyanne

lips parted. Before Jordan could reach up to pull him closer, Trey moved. Their mouths came together and everything that wasn't Trey faded from Jordan's awareness.

Quicker than a blink, sparks flared in Jordan's blood. In seconds, passion's fire consumed him. Hard, possessive hands took his hips and pulled him forward. Jordan's arms slid around Trey's broad shoulders. He moaned, he couldn't help it. It was pure Heaven to be in Trey's arms again.

When Trey pulled away, Jordan almost cursed in frustration. He opened his eyes to see Trey staring at something over his shoulder. He tried to turn around, but Trey's arms tightened around him. Jordan realized in a rush that Trey was down on one knee. Jordan was straddling the raised one and was practically wrapped around Trey.

"So, umm, I guess you decided to leave the hotel."

Recognizing the agent's voice, Jordan struggled to stand up. Trey refused to release him. Instead, he pushed to his feet while keeping one arm locked around Jordan's waist. The slide of Trey's thigh against his ass cheeks drew a moan he had to fight to hold inside. His arms dropped from around Trey's shoulders. One hand rested against Trey's chest to maintain his balance.

When they were both standing, Trey still wouldn't let go. He kept them pressed together from chest to thigh as if daring the agent to mention it. Tension curled in the air.

"I thought I told you to say away from Jordan."

"Actually, I came by because everyone recommended the diner as the best place to grab a bite. I didn't know his family owned it."

Trey snorted. "Yes, you did, just a convenient loophole. I didn't tell you to leave his family alone."

"He is standing right here." Jordan forced Trey to release him and turned so he could see both of the other men. "Why did you want to talk to me? And, why did you tell him not to? " His first question was for the agent, not that he cared one way or the other as he would refuse to discuss Trey with anyone. As for the second question, he definitely wanted that answer.

"His contract is under negotiation at the moment. It's a tricky business and a competitive one. I need to make sure you aren't going to cause any problems for him."

"Goddammit, Silas, it's none of your business."

"Your contract is every bit my business. That's the most important part of my job."

"This isn't about my contract."

"The hell it's not," Silas argued. "You think the Wildcats won't have something to say about their QB's life choices?"

"My personal life isn't any of their business or yours for that matter."

"Oh, get real, Trey. If you believed that you wouldn't be hiding your little puff piece behind the diner."

Jordan stepped in front of Trey, blocking him from going after the agent. He addressed Silas. "You don't have anything to worry about from me. I've been protecting Trey a lot longer than you have."

Trey moved around Jordan and pointed at him and then at Silas while he fought against his anger.

"I don't need protecting, not by either of you. I'm a grown man who can make his own decisions." Trey's furious glare pinned Jordan. "I have been for a long time." His eyes flew back to Silas. "And if you ever call him that again, I'll throat punch you."

"I think you boys need something to cool down." Tavia Brooks gave pointed looks to each man before handing Jordan a tray with three glasses. "I won't lie and say I wasn't eavesdropping, but the customers haven't heard you. Yet. But, if you keep raising your voices, it's only a matter of time.

"Trey, honey, it's so good to see you. It's been far too long." She hugged Trey and took his arm. "Danny's waiting for you to come in and sign the jersey. I don't mean to rush you, but he had a stroke about a month back and he still tires easily so if you don't mind..."

"No ma'am I don't mind, but..." Trey darted a glance at Jordan and then a glare at Silas.

"My boy can handle himself," Tavia said and tugged Trey toward the back door of the diner.

Jordan watched them disappear inside and then turned his attention to Silas. He read the speculation in the other man's eyes and kept his own face expressionless.

"So you're the reason he fought coming back here. He wasn't very happy when I suggested it."

"I'm sure it had nothing to do with me," Jordan denied. "He always wanted out of Avery. Swore he'd never come back if he got away. He's been pretty good at avoiding this place for twenty years."

"That embrace didn't look like nothing."

"If you're fishing, you forgot your bait. I have nothing at all to tell you about Trey except he's a damn good athlete and deserves every accolade he's ever gotten."

"You could ruin him."

Jordan almost laughed at that. "I doubt that, but in any case, you needn't worry. I've kept his secret for two decades. If I wanted five minutes of fame, I've had plenty of time to get it. The problem now is that you know. It's no longer a secret just between him and me. You are the weak link."

"Never happen. I'm his agent. It's part of my job to keep his image immaculate."

"And what happens if you get drunk one night and spill the beans? Or, you get mad at him because he turns down a deal that you busted your ass to put together? Or, you sign someone younger straight out of college? Once it's out there, it can't be taken back."

"Hurting Trey would hurt me."

"Financially, yeah. You've got a lot invested in him at the moment. But things like that change." Jordan sighed. "Look, I'm not into pissing contests. I kept Trey's secret when he didn't have anything but determination and his God-given ability. I'm not going to do anything that would cause him to lose his career."

"So, it doesn't bother you that he left you here in the sticks while he's out there living the high life?"

Jordan's laugh was hollow. "I severed the ties between us so I wouldn't hold him back. It damn near killed me, but it was best for him. Like I said, you don't have anything to fear from me." Jordan turned his back on the agent to hide the sadness he could no longer suppress. "If you'll excuse me, I have meat to check."

"You still love him."

Three days ago, Jordan would have said no. After seeing Trey again, he knew he would have been lying.

"Always."

Chapter Twelve
~ * ~ * ~

Trey capped the Sharpie and handed it back to Jordan's dad. "There ya go, Mr. B. You want me to help you put it back in the frame and hang it up?"

"Nah, we need to make sure it dries so it doesn't smear. Tavi and I will get it like we did last time."

"I can't believe you dedicated a whole wall of the diner to me. I think you may have more pictures of me than my mom."

"If I have one she doesn't, I'll make her a copy." Mr. Brooks smiled at him, and Trey noted the effects of the stroke. Jordan hadn't said anything about it last night, but then, they had other issues that needed to be resolved.

"I don't mean to rush out, but I have a few things I need to talk to Jordan about before I leave."

Mr. Brooks laid a hand on Trey's arm. When Trey looked at the older man, he saw a great sadness in the man's eyes.

"The decision he made wasn't easy for him."

"The decision to leave me?" Trey didn't try to disguise the hurt in his voice. The anger. "The decision he won't tell me about. What happened?"

Mr. Brooks shook his head. "I promised him I wouldn't tell you and so did his mother. We tried to change his mind, but…just take it easy on him, okay. It took him a very long time to get where he is now."

Frustrated, Trey pulled away from the older man's touch. "It would be a lot easier if someone would tell me what the hell happened."

Mr. Brooks bent over the small office desk and shuffled some papers around before he scribbled something on a piece of paper. "You want to know, then you keep asking him. That's his number." Mr. Brooks shoved the scrap of paper into Trey's hand. "But, you didn't get that from me."

Trey tucked the paper in his pocket. He wasn't going to need a number, he intended to clear the air before he left. He just had to get Silas out of the picture.

When he stepped out of the small office, he knew things weren't going to happen as planned. A small roar came from the seating area. Mrs. Brooks gave him a sheepish smile and pointed toward the front of the diner. A crowd had gathered.

"Word got out that you were here. Some of the town folks wanted to know if you had time to sign autographs before you go. You can duck out the back if you'd rather not."

The last thing he wanted to do was get tangled up with fans while his emotions were skipping all over the place. Anywhere else, he probably would have refused, but Avery was different. Avery was home. Trey forced a smile to curve his lips.

"Sure thing, Mrs. B."

Relief shone in her eyes. "I'll let your friend know; I believe he's still out back with Jordan."

Trey's attention immediately shifted to the back door of the diner. He took a step toward it. Jordan's mother stepped into his path. Her face softened a bit and she shook her head. Trey's shoulders slumped. He knew she was right. There were too many eyes and ears around. Resigned, he turned back to the seating area.

Two hours passed in a blur of faces, young and old. Silas joined him bringing trading cards and glossy headshots for Trey to sign. When they all disappeared, Trey posed for pictures with adults and children, held babies decked out in Wildcat onesies and recounted numerous stories about the two championship seasons he'd had at the high school, his college years and life as a Wildcat.

Mr. Brooks brought him a plate with a huge pulled pork sandwich, corn on the cob and mac and cheese. Mrs. Brooks kept his glass full and brought him cookies. Janice came in for her shift near the end, glared at him for a second and then cut a path straight to the kitchen. Jordan never showed his face. Trey knew because he searched for the other man in the milling crowd.

"Okay, everyone. I'm afraid we have to go." Silas waited for the noise to die down. "I hope Trey was able to sign something for everyone. I know I've enjoyed meeting all of you. It's been a great trip back home for him."

Trey gained his feet intent on finding Jordan, but Silas grabbed him by the elbow. He leaned over and whispered. "Pilot's doing pre-flight. We need to get on the road."

Trey jerked his arm free. "Pretty damn convenient, you get to talk to Jordan and the jet is suddenly all clear. It can wait. I haven't finished my talk with him."

"He's gone."

"You don't know that."

"I watched him leave, Trey. And now, we have to go. I've already rescheduled the ESPN interview for later tonight. I can't change it again."

Short of making a scene, Trey had little choice except to wave and smile at the small crowd who followed them outside. Jordan's parents hugged him. Mr. Brooks invited him to come back whenever he could.

~*~*~

J.T. Cheyanne

"Are you going to be an ass all the way back to New York?" Silas merely raised an eyebrow at Trey's scowl. "You didn't even want to come back here, remember?"

Trey flung himself into the airplane seat and buckled the seat belt. He hadn't wanted to come, but after seeing Jordan, he didn't want to leave. That kiss behind the diner had ripped open a hole inside of him that he wasn't sure he could close again. Memories long locked away seeped through the ragged edges.

But, there was no way he was spilling any of that to Silas so he plugged his headphones into his ears and closed his eyes. They were not going to have the argument he could see brewing all over Silas's face.

With the familiar growl of Disturbed playing in his ears, his mind drifted to Jordan, or rather back to Jordan. Not surprising. Jordan had consumed his thoughts since Trey had spotted him at the high school. No longer the shy, insecure teenager Trey remembered, Jordan had matured, gained confidence and Trey guessed life had not been easy on him. Shadows clouded Jordan's eyes. They hadn't been there before. A quiet strength radiated from the other man and Trey was sure the shadows were the cause.

Add stubbornness. In spades. That was definitely new. When they were dating, Jordan had never been able to keep secrets from Trey. A few kisses and he could persuade Jordan to tell him anything. But, whatever had caused Jordan to change his mind about them, Jordan was keeping it close to his chest even after a couple of kisses. It had affected both of their lives, and Trey wasn't about to let it go. Jordan owed him an explanation. Trey intended to get it, especially after that second kiss.

Everything about the kiss confused him. He was angry at Jordan. And hurt. He had carted that anger and hurt around for years. Too often, he used it as a mantle to keep others away. It had been an effective barrier that even Silas hadn't been able to penetrate. But, every time Jordan got close, the pain and anger floated away like feathers floating in the wind.

Jordan's mouth, the taste of him, the feel of him sliding into Trey's arms felt natural and right. Yet, the harmony was bittersweet. That first year away at college, he'd lain awake too many nights to count longing for Jordan and just one more chance, one more kiss. He thought he'd left all of that behind him. But, now that he'd gotten close to Jordan again his libido had taken over. All he wanted to do was get his hands, mouth, whatever he could, on the man. It was as if the intervening years hadn't happened.

The clash of hot and cold inside of him was confusing. His chest ached. His stomach rolled. Anger warred against lust. Hurt battled against longing. And, he still didn't have any answers to help sort through the chaos.

Chapter Thirteen
~ * ~ * ~

The tardy bell screeched its warning across the school grounds as Jordan bailed out of his car and hurried to the entrance. He hated being late, but after a fretful night spent tossing and turning, he'd slept through his alarm. To make matters worse, the car keys had played a spectacular game of hide-and-seek and Mother Nature had iced the streets.

A few steps from the door, a massive wave of sirens and whistles erupted from his pocket. He very nearly cursed out loud. With his computer bag barely clinging to his shoulder and his glasses sliding down his nose, he reached for the door with one hand and dug his phone out with the other. He slid his thumb across the bottom without looking at the number and put the phone to his ear.

"Hang on."

He sent an apologetic look to the vice principal on duty in the foyer and rushed through the office to check-in for the day. In the hall again, he put the phone back to his ear and adjusted the strap on his shoulder.

"Hello?"

"I didn't interrupt anything did I?"

Jordan stopped so suddenly the shoulder strap slid right back off of his shoulder. The bag hit the floor. One teacher poked her head out of her classroom and frowned.

"Trey?" Shock catapulted his voice two octaves higher than normal. It had been two weeks since the reunion. Two weeks of sleepless nights spent tossing and turning. Two weeks of 'what ifs' and daydreaming about kisses behind the diner. Two Sundays of torturing himself by watching Trey play football.

"Yeah, it's me. You sound out of breath."

"I'm late for work." Jordan ducked into the boys' bathroom, dragging his bag by the strap.

"Damn, I forgot about the time difference. I have to leave for practice in an hour so I thought, never mind. It's not a good time for either of us."

"Trey, listen, I…"

"No, you listen," Trey interrupted. "The game Sunday is in Colorado. We're flying out of Philly on Thursday. I'm going to have a ticket for you at Will Call."

"I can't…"

"Yes, you can," Trey interrupted again.

"Would you just listen?" The frustration in Jordan's voice must have carried through the line because Trey remained quiet.

"I don't have time to argue with you about this. I have to get to my classroom. I have students waiting for me."

"Fine. Call me when you get home."

Jordan didn't want to make that promise. He hesitated.

"Call me, or I'll just keep calling you. I want to know what happened, Jordan. Seeing you again…I haven't been able to sleep. I can't stop thinking about you. About us."

Trey's raspy voice conveyed pain and confusion. Anguish knotted in Jordan's stomach. He closed his eyes and fought the surge of emotion. "Trey that was so long ago. We have lives, careers; we're different now. Men instead of teenagers."

"That kiss behind the diner didn't feel different. It felt right." And, because it had felt the same for him, Jordan relented.

"I'll call you, but I really, really have to go."

"Swear."

"You know I don't do that."

"Promise me, then."

Gods, how many times had they had that exact same exchange? He found himself smiling as he responded. "Fine, I promise."

"And, you always keep…" Trey's words cut off abruptly. "Bye, Jordan."

The phone call ended abruptly. Jordan's smile faded. 'You always keep your promises.' That was supposed to be the final line. But, he hadn't kept the last promise. The most important one of their lives. Utterly deflated, he shoved the phone back in his pocket.

In the classroom, he went through roll call and the other necessary morning paperwork by rote. The bell rang, students scurried out to their first classes and more filtered in for his class. He forced himself to focus and opened the math book to the lesson for the day. For the first time in his life, the numbers and words in the Algebra text swam before his eyes in a meaningless sea of unrecognizable shapes and lines.

~*~*~

"I didn't think you would call."

"I promised I would."

For a long moment, Trey didn't respond. "So, you're a school teacher. Let me guess. P.E.?"

In spite of the anxiety eating a hole in his gut, Jordan smiled. "Oh yeah, you know it. The kid who yelled 'score a touchdown' at the basketball game is definitely in charge of physical education."

"Second guess, math."

"Got it in two. Algebra one and two, pre-cal, calculus one and two, geometry, for grades nine through twelve. I have an AP course for the college-bound, too."

"They're lucky to have you. You were always a fantastic tutor. I wouldn't have passed without your help."

"I, uh, thank you. You were easy to tutor. You were motivated."

The conversation lulled. Jordan could hear Trey breathing on the other end. He tried to think of something to say and fell back on an oldie from their high school days.

"Practice go okay?"

"Yeah, we watched some film, had our mistakes pointed out. Hit the gym for a workout, took a few snaps. Nothing out of the ordinary. How was school, Teach?"

Honestly, Jordan didn't have a clue how he'd made it through the day. He couldn't escape the memories. Other than fresh paint and more computers, the school remained relatively the same as when they had attended classes together. The dam holding back the flood had burst when Trey walked through the door of the boy's locker room and Jordan was drowning in the onslaught.

Everywhere he looked, he saw Trey. The water fountain where he stood waiting for Trey to pass so their eyes could meet just that split second between classes. Trey's old locker right across the hall from Jordan's classroom. The trophy case in the foyer with two state championship trophies and Trey's high school football picture. Jordan had worn the jersey shown in that picture and nothing else. It had smelled of sweat and Trey. The gym where he'd watched Trey play basketball, the nights spent at the football and baseball fields.

He'd even caught a glimpse of the field house where Trey had stolen more than a few kisses in the shadows after a game. His large body and the dark corner had blocked Jordan from sight. Heat scalded his cheeks as he remembered that hard, muscular body, sweaty and slick from the game pressed into him, caging him in the corner while Trey's mouth plundered his. They'd been fools to take those chances, but he hadn't been capable of telling Trey to stop.

"Jordan?"

With a gulp, he realized he'd gone down the rabbit hole again.

"I'm here."

"Was school that bad?"

"Uh, no. It was just a regular day." Of daydreaming about the hot quarterback. Gods, how many useless days had he spent doing just that? Every one of them his senior year for sure. "The kids are still talking about your visit. They are really putting in some thought on how to use the money you donated."

"I can't wrap my head around the fact you're a teacher. You wanted to work for NASA. MIT sent a representative to your house."

"Things didn't turn out like I'd planned, that's for sure."

"One day you're going to tell me why."

Jordan's fingers tightened on the phone. His mouth went dry. Why couldn't Trey just let it go? Neither of them would benefit from digging in the past.

When Jordan remained quiet, Trey changed the subject.

"How's Mr. B?"

"Getting better every day. They've cut back on the rehab. Thanks for signing the jersey; he's over the moon about that."

"Not a problem." Trey went quiet. Jordan was content just listening to him breathe, but that wasn't going to accomplish much. He started to speak only to have Trey break the silence first.

"Jordan, I want you to come to Colorado for the game. I need to see you again."

Jordan's heart stuttered. "Why?"

"I want to know what happened. I need answers. I tried to put all of that behind me. I thought I was right where I wanted to be in life. But when I saw you in the parking lot Friday, shoving your glasses back up on your nose...," Trey's voice caught and he stopped, took a deep breath.

"I realized that my life has been on pause for twenty years."

"Trey, that's not true. You have everything you always dreamed about."

"Damn it, Jordie, stop telling me that." Trey's anger raced through the phone to slap at him. Jordan shrank into the sofa and closed his eyes. But, Trey wasn't finished.

"I think you're trying to convince yourself that it's true so you don't feel guilty. It's not true, not for me. I dreamed about more than football and fame. I dreamed about love and family. I wanted, still want, what our parents had. I wanted that with you. I thought you wanted the same thing." Hurt and betrayal laced the last words. They broke the fragile pieces of Jordan's taped together heart.

"I did," Jordan whispered. There was no way he could deny that and cause Trey even more pain. "I do. But, it wasn't meant for us. You wouldn't be in the pros now if you'd come out back then."

"That was my decision to make, our decision, if you prefer. It wasn't yours alone. You let me believe we had a future."

"I wanted that future, Trey. Believe me, I did."

"Then come to Colorado and tell me what happened. Tell me why you bailed on us."

"It's not going to change anything, Trey."

"You don't know that." Trey sighed. Jordan could imagine him shoving his fingers through his hair, something he always did when he was upset.

"I'm pushing play here, Jordan. I'm putting whatever was between us into motion again. The kiss at the hotel and the one behind the diner, it felt like we'd never been apart. You said you aren't in a relationship. I'll have the ticket at Will Call. If you can't afford the airfare, I'll pay for it. Excuse the sports analogy, but the ball's in your court."

In a much quieter voice, he continued. "I need you to come, Jordie. Please."

His heart melted. Tears burned his eyes. How could he resist the plea in Trey's voice? Did he even want to ignore it?

It would be easier to just say no, to avoid all of the painful memories the trip would dredge up, to avoid the chance of both of them being hurt all over again, to avoid the hiding and sneaking around again. Jordan wanted more than a boyfriend in the shadows, but was Trey ready for that type of commitment, or the spotlight that would glare at him?

Jordan cleared his throat. "I'll see if I can get a sub for Friday, but it's really short notice. And, there may not be any flights available."

Trey didn't respond. Even through the phone, Jordan sensed the tension in Trey. Or maybe, it was the tension squeezing his chest. His heart yearned to go, but the realist in his brain hesitated.

"I'll, um, I can check and let you know tomorrow. I have some papers to grade and a few college recommendation letters to write out."

"I won't give up, Jordan. If you don't make this game, there will be others. The season will end. I'll be free to come back to Avery. I'm not going to stay away this time. We are going to have this conversation. Go and grade your papers, and when you get done, dream about me."

In the next breath, the phone clicked off and Trey was gone.

Jordan dropped his phone onto the sofa beside him. His head fell back on the cushion. After days, weeks, months and years of wondering what would happen if he saw Trey again, Fate was giving him the answer. Trey was still interested. Furious with him, but still interested. He wanted to talk, to pick up where they'd ended. All Jordan had to do was gather his courage and take the leap. He wasn't sure he could he do that. He'd barely survived losing Trey the first time.

Jordan pushed to his feet and wandered into the kitchen. Memories buffeted the doubts running rampant in his head. Love battered against logic. Hope danced into the fray taking aim at reticence with deadly accuracy.

If he went, there was no way to avoid telling Trey the truth. Jordan tasted the bitterness of fear at the back of his throat. Anger could very easily turn to disgust. The tentative spark could be snuffed out with only a few words.

Unable to settle, he made himself a cup of hot tea, added a spoonful of sugar and wrapped his hands around the mug. Warmth seeped into his palms. He carried it in to the living room and sat down again. His thoughts twisted like snakes.

Trey's life had gone exactly as he'd planned, and Jordan was truly glad of that fact. His life, however, had veered into disaster. Trey seemed to believe Jordan had simply gotten scared and changed his mind. He had been scared, but it hadn't kept him from leaving Avery. How many times had he wished things had turned out differently? What if he'd left earlier in the day? What if he'd just flown out with Trey? What if he'd just let his parents call Trey?

What ifs didn't change things; they only drove a person crazy. Jordan set the mug aside, tugged his glasses free and rubbed his stinging eyes. After a deep breath, he replaced them and stared at the stacks of test papers and homework in front of him. The red marker lay on the middle pile. He leaned forward, but instead of reaching for the pen, he grabbed the cell and hit the Google search tab.

~*~*~

After making the arrangements for the ticket for Jordan, Trey tossed the phone onto the bed. The fluffy duvet muffled any sound it might have made. Trey scrubbed both hands though his hair. The silence of the hotel room beat against his ears. Alone. The same as always.

Was that why he'd asked Jordan to come to the game? He hadn't intended to when he'd answered the call. He wasn't really sure what he'd expected. He just knew he hadn't been able to push Jordan far from his thoughts.

At practices, he caught himself gazing at the sidelines remembering a skinny kid keeping stats for a game he never fully understood. Alone in the hotel room, he couldn't concentrate on game plans or game film. The scab covering his deepest hurt had been snatched away. The hurt and anger of that lonely teenage boy flowed free, demanded answers to ease the suffering soul.

Grabbing a towel from the rack in the bathroom, he headed downstairs to the hotel gym. He was both surprised and relieved to find the space empty. After choosing a treadmill, he programmed a good cardiovascular workout. Earbuds in his ears, he pegged the start button and eased into the run.

The music did little to drown out his thoughts which reverted right back to Jordan. He needed answers because it had become painfully clear that he wasn't as over Jordan as he'd thought. The kiss in the hotel room had been purely instinct. His body had responded to the familiar, his heart to the boy he'd loved. The reaction had blindsided him. Behind the diner, the kiss had been deliberate. He had to see if it had been a fluke. It hadn't. He still wanted to strangle Silas for interrupting them.

What the hell had happened? Janice and Mr. B had both alluded to pain in Jordan's past. It drove him crazy not knowing the hows and whys. If Jordan actually showed up, he'd have three days to pry the answers out of him.

Chapter Fourteen
~ * ~ * ~

Jordan sat on the edge of the bed staring down at the phone in his hand. He'd saved Trey's number but hadn't actually used it. He wanted to, but nerves kept him from actually hitting the button to put the call through. He'd considered texting, but he wouldn't be able to hear Trey's voice that way. Plus, it was rather impersonal and they had a lot of very personal stuff to talk about.

He still hadn't decided what he was going to tell Trey. Janice and his parents believed full disclosure was best. Jordan didn't quite agree. Dragging all of the skeletons out of the closet wouldn't change the past. He wasn't sure it could change the present.

The jarring ring of the cell screamed into the silence. It startled Jordan so badly he juggled the device before dropping it. It bounced across the carpet. He fumbled to pick it up while shoving his glasses onto his nose. Of course, the blasted thing ended up under the bed. Jordan bent to retrieve it, lost his balance and cracked his head against the corner of the bedside table. His glasses slid off of his nose and tumbled to the floor, leaving everything hazy.

Cursing under his breath, he patted around under the bed until he found the still blaring phone and pulled it out. Snagging his glasses with his other hand, he sat back on his heels and thumbed the green blur on the screen.

"Hello?"

"Jordan? You okay? You sound out of breath."

Trey. As if he were conjured by Jordan's thoughts. Jordan slid his glasses back on and rubbed the sore spot on his forehead.

"Um, yeah. I'm fine. I dropped the phone. It went under the bed. I lost my glasses when I bent over to get it. I was just about to call you. Well, I was debating between a call and a text, because I wasn't sure if you were in practice or not. And, I'm rambling." Jordan pressed his lips together.

"I'm not complaining." Trey's chuckle rumbled in Jordan's ear. It carried with it warmth and familiarity. Memories of sneaking away on summer days to swim in the river, of late-night phone calls snuggled in bed with the phone pressed to his ear wishing Trey was there with him. Places inside of him that had been locked down for years loosened. The invisible bonds of grief and sadness frayed but didn't give up their hold.

"I missed you." Jordan winced and bit his lip. He hadn't meant to say that out loud. How pathetic did it sound?

J.T. Cheyanne

"Not enough apparently, or you would have called instead of just thinking about it." Trey stopped and Jordan could hear him take a breath. "I'm sorry. I need to let go of this anger, but it's not easy."

"It's okay. I can understand why you're angry. I hurt you, so I kind of expected it."

"I want to understand what happened, but that's not going to happen if I keep bashing you every time I talk to you." Another deep breath. "So, have you given any thought to coming out for the game?"

"Actually, I'm, ah, already here. That's why I was going to call."

"What?!" Jordan held the phone away from his ear as Trey's voice gained volume. "When did you get in? Why didn't' you let me know? I could have picked you up at the airport. Where are you staying? I can come over."

"You don't have to do that. It's late. I know you didn't expect me to be here so early and you probably had practice today so I know you're tired. They had a seat available so I flew out right after school. I was definitely going to call you tomorrow and tell you I was here. You get some sleep. We're both tired."

"Where are you?"

Jordan recognized that tone. Trey had made up his mind and there wouldn't be any changing it. "The DoubleTree on Quebec Street."

"You're not that far. It'll be about fifteen minutes. I just need to get dressed and get a taxi."

The image of Trey stretched out across a bed, naked, stole every bit of Jordan's breath. Before he could tell him not to come, the phone disconnected. Jordan looked helplessly at the home screen of his cell before dashing for the shower.

~*~*~

In the hallway outside of Jordan's hotel room, Trey stared at the door. He lifted his hand to knock but dropped it back to his side. Again. He hated the uncertainty that stayed his hand, but he'd never been more nervous in his life. Not at the state championship games, not his first start as a college athlete or even his first snap as a professional football player. He supposed it was because he never doubted his ability to play the game. He was always prepared to handle any situation on the field.

What lay on the other side of the door? Jordan, of course. And answers to questions that had plagued his entire adult life. A man whose ghost had haunted his dreams. He had to admit that Jordan was right in one respect. He'd never come out because of his profession. And, while he hadn't been celibate, he hadn't been true to himself either. Would things have been different if he had come out? Would Jordan have made a different decision about them?

J.T. Cheyanne

The "what ifs" drove him nuts. There was only one way to get them answered. He knocked. The door swung open almost immediately. The smile on Jordan's face faltered.

"Oh, wow! You're fast."

Trey shrugged. "So are you. I barely finished knocking."

Jordan's face flushed. "I thought you were room service. I haven't had anything to eat since I landed. I ordered a burger for you." He shrugged self-consciously as his gaze darted away. "I know you don't eat much after practice so I ordered a salad, too, so you can choose."

"I can't believe you remember that."

Jordan stepped back and waved him into the room. "Of course, I remember. I think you ate dinner at the diner every night after practice our senior year."

"Because you were there."

Jordan's eyes closed and his head fell forward. Both arms wound around his waist as if holding himself together. It wasn't the defensive pose Trey remembered from the bullying in high school. Rather, it spoke of deep pain. He reached out, but let his hand fall before it made contact. If Jordan noticed, he didn't comment.

"It seems that was our place." Jordan finally spoke.

"Yeah." Trey prowled around the room, hands shoved in the pockets of his track pants. Nerves kept him on his feet. "You still work there?"

Jordan shook his head as he moved away from the door. "Not really. I've been filling in since dad had the stroke, but mostly they keep the teenagers employed. Not much else to do in Avery."

Trey nodded. "That hasn't changed much. I'm surprised you're still there. I always thought you wanted to leave as bad as I did. When you didn't show up, I thought you'd decided to go to MIT."

"I never applied to MIT." Shock brought Trey's head up. Jordan sat on the bed. He shrugged one shoulder. "It would have been a waste of paperwork and time. I did one application and got accepted. I eventually followed you to Rutgers, about ten years after you graduated."

"So you worked at the diner until then?"

"No. Well, sort of. Off and on." Jordan's shoulders hunched into the defensive position Trey did remember. What was he hiding?

"You aren't making any sense. The day I left, I thought we had everything planned. I even expected to see you at the airport. I should have known then something was wrong."

Jordan shoved up off of the bed. "I was at the diner the day you left for college. I wanted to go to the airport, but I knew it would be too hard. I wouldn't be able to hug you, or kiss you. It hurt knowing I wouldn't be able to say goodbye like everyone else. I nearly went crazy. I couldn't get

J.T. Cheyanne

the orders right; I burned the burgers. I don't know how many drinks I spilled before Mom and Dad sent me home. And, that was even worse. There wasn't anything to distract me, nothing to take away the ache inside."

"You should've come to the airport."

"And, do what, Trey? Stand in the crowd and watch you leave while pretending everything was fine? Don't you think people would have noticed if I'd been by your side? People didn't even know we were friends, much less more than that. I was just your tutor, a tool to get you into college."

Trey's temper spiked. "You were more than that and you know it."

"I do know it. But your parents didn't. The media didn't. Your teammates didn't. You weren't ready for them to know."

It was Trey's turn to be defensive. "You said you understood."

"I did." Frustration marred Jordan's features. "I still do. That's why I had to stay at home."

"That's why you didn't come when the term started." Trey was incredulous.

"No." Jordan tunneled his fingers through his hair and paced toward the bed again. He sat on the edge and popped right back up. He looked at Trey. Pain, regret and something else flickered in the depths of his eyes. Suddenly, Trey wasn't so sure he wanted to know.

"Did you meet someone else that summer?" Even to his own ears, his voice sounded strangled.

Jordan's laugh was anything but mirthful. His eyes dropped down to inspect the carpet. "No. Not for a long, long time after you were gone."

"Did someone…hurt you?" Trey's stomach revolted at the thought. None of the football team had teased Jordan after Trey had beat the shit out of Parker and tossed him in the dumpster. Everyone knew Trey was leaving. Had his absence left Jordan open to a bully?

"Yes."

Trey's world ground to a halt.

"But not the way you're thinking. It wasn't anyone in Avery."

A knock on the door interrupted them. Trey cursed while Jordan swiped at his face. "I got it." Trey strode to the door and made quick work of getting rid of the bellhop. He rolled the trolley close to the bed and picked up the bottled water. He offered it to Jordan.

"Thanks." Jordan cracked the seal and took a long swallow. He flashed a quick look at Trey. "Maybe, we should eat first."

"The food can wait. I finally got you talking; I don't want you to stop. What happened, Jordie?"

J.T. Cheyanne

Jordan sighed, shoulders slumped. "I was coming, Trey. I marked off every day on the calendar before I went to bed. When we hung up that last time, I finished packing what was left in my room. The car was loaded with everything I owned. Mom and Dad even gave me a bonus check from the diner to help pay for gas."

"But, you never left Avery."

"Oh, I left." Jordan fled to the windows. His movements, tight and jerky, appeared almost robotic. He stared out into the darkness. Trey crossed the room and went with instinct. He circled Jordan with his arms and stepped in close enough for their bodies to brush. It felt like the most natural thing in the world, having Jordan in his arms. A slight pressure at his hips and Jordan's body pressed back into him. He rested his laced fingers on Jordan's abdomen. It scared him to feel how hard Jordan's body trembled in his embrace.

"Jordan?"

The words finally came, slow and stilted. "I was about a hundred miles out of Avery, scared to death and excited at the same time. I had so many ideas running through my head, things we could do, places to visit around the university, quiet time with just you and me and no parents."

Jordan shifted but didn't move away. Trey waited for him to continue. A sense of dread formed a lump in his throat.

"A drunk driver ran a stop sign and hit me. It was bad. We were in the middle of nowhere. I don't know how long it was before someone found us and called 911. I was in and out of consciousness. I barely remember the ambulance ride. Mom and Dad came, of course."

Trey watched Jordan's reflection in the glass. Fear. Pain. Grief. Sadness. Things he'd seen before and wanted to wipe away.

"You called them, but you didn't call me."

Jordan broke Trey's embrace and moved away. "Actually, the police contacted my parents, and then the hospital."

"They knew about us, your parents, they knew. Why didn't they call me?"

"At first, because they were so worried about me. Life Flight was called. I was air-lifted to Jackson. They didn't know how bad it was because no one would tell them anything." Jordan turned and met his gaze fully. "Later, when the dust finally settled, I told them not to. I made them promise they wouldn't call you and that they wouldn't talk to you if you called. Don't blame them."

"But, your mom…"

Jordan's head dropped. "Mom shouldn't have lied to you. The vacation thing was her idea. She wanted to give you something to hang on to because she could hear in your voice that you were hurting. She hoped

I would change my mind and believe me, she tried to make that happen. They both did. But, just like you said the last time we talked, you would have come back to Avery. It would have ruined your scholarship, your future."

Trey's temper spiked again. "God damn it, Jordan, it was our future. Football wasn't my life. You were. I could have red-shirted, or changed schools."

"You don't know that," Jordan shot back. "What if you'd come back and lost your chance to play? You'd have been stuck in Avery, a place you hated. Eventually, you would have hated me."

"And what if you're wrong? Maybe, I was good enough the coach would have waited one more year." Which wasn't fair, Trey knew. His coach had told him to forget his high school sweetheart and explore the brand new wide-open world. But, Jordan didn't know that.

"One more year and the next wave of high school graduates would be on the market. I may not like football, or even understand the game, but I know that for every player that gets a scholarship, there are hundreds more who would love to take his place."

Trey knew the truth of those words, but it didn't ease the heartache. "It wasn't your decision to make, Jordan. You didn't even give me a chance to talk about it. What if you'd died and I never knew? I loved you more than anything else in the world, even football. You just brushed my feelings aside like I didn't matter."

"That's not true," Jordan denied.

"Yes, it is." Trey refused to give ground. "And after you got out of the hospital? You still didn't call, or show up. If you loved me like you said, how could you just let me go so easily?"

"It wasn't easy. Never think that. It is still one of the hardest things I've had to do in my life. I lay in that damn hospital bed and cried for hours. I mourned the loss of us."

"That was your own fault." Jordan's body jerked at the harshness in Trey's voice. "I would have been there if I'd known. You didn't have to be alone. Apparently, I had a lot more faith in us than you did."

"Maybe you did, but we can't change the past. We've talked about it and nothing is any different. You're still angry, and I still believe I made the right choice. It was a waste of time to come out here."

"So, you're going to tuck your tail and run away again?"

Jordan twisted around to glare at him. "I didn't run away the first time. I've lived my entire life in one place. You knew where to find me."

"Why would I come back where I wasn't wanted?"

"I don't know, Trey. Why did you come back after all this time? And, we both know it wasn't to see me so don't even attempt that one."

"I didn't want to see anyone. It was all Silas's idea. The check to the school, the docu-whatever thing he filmed. It was all because my contract is up for renewal and he thought it would look good in the press. I couldn't refuse without looking like an ass."

"So it was Silas who told you to give me the keycard?"

Trey flushed. "Uh, no, that was all on me."

"Why?"

Trey debated the answer and decided on the truth. He couldn't lie to Jordan when he was demanding truth from the other man.

"I don't know. I saw you when we were leaving the school. You were in the parking lot, going home I guess. At first, your back was to me so I wasn't sure, but then you turned and shoved your glasses up on your nose the way you used to when we were studying."

Jordan's gaze darted away. A dull flush darkened his cheeks. Trey knew he was remembering the same thing he had. The teasing and the stolen kisses. The laughter and the love.

"That heartbroken kid inside of me stirred around and woke up. I realized that I wanted the answers to the "what ifs" and you were the only one who had them."

"I had a panic attack when I saw you."

"You still have those?"

"Apparently, though it's been years since the last one." Jordan stopped pacing and sat down on the edge of the bed. His shoulders slumped.

"I was an eighteen-year-old kid, Trey. In pain, scared, and trying to do what I thought was best for the boy I loved. I didn't want you to lose your dream. I didn't want to be the rock around your neck that kept you in Avery."

"And you couldn't tell me all of that back then?"

"To what purpose?" Jordan flared. "There's a few what-if questions you're forgetting or you choose to ignore, Trey." Jordan crossed the room and stood right in front of him. "What if I did call you and everyone found out you had a boyfriend? What if they weren't very accepting of a gay freshman quarterback? If you were so upset and worried about me why didn't you come back to Avery on your first school break?

"It's been twenty years, and you're still firmly in the closet. Do you think I would have been happy living in your shadow, hiding from the press? Maybe, if I'd been Sunny Debona, head cheerleader and prom queen things would have been different?"

Trey didn't know what to say. He had thought about how things would have been different if Jordan had been with him. But, had he fully considered how it would have affected Jordan? Taking advantage of his silence, Jordan stepped away and turned his back.

"I'm tired, Trey, and you probably have another day of game prep to get through tomorrow. Let's just call it a night."

"Are you going to leave in the morning?"

Jordan was silent for a long minute before shaking his head. "No. Let me know when you get out of practice, maybe we can do…something, maybe try to talk again."

Trey didn't want to leave, but he could tell Jordan had shut down. He went to the door and opened it, paused and looked back over his shoulder. Jordan stood once again with his head down and his arms wrapped tightly around his middle.

"Night, Jordie. Sleep well." He waited a breath. "Dream of me."

"I always do."

The choked whisper slipped through the door just before it closed. It arrowed straight into Trey's chest and found his wounded heart. Surprisingly, instead of hurting, a soft warmth bloomed.

Chapter Fifteen
~ * ~ * ~

"I'm proud of you, Jordan Brooks. You shouldn't take all of the blame."

"But, it was mostly my fault."

Janice growled. "Stop it, you imbecile. It takes two make a relationship work and he didn't follow through either."

"He had his hands full with a new team, practice, starting college."

"And you've always made excuses for him. It's about time you made him face some hard facts. He really expected you to live all of your life like you did in Avery? Hiding from the world? What kind of life would you have had?"

"One with him."

"I've told you over and over; it would have been a half-life; always waiting for him to come home. It's not like he could take you to the games or stuff. People would notice, and he couldn't have that."

"I know you're right, and that's one of the reasons I left things the way they were when it was all over. But, seeing him again, it's all still in there, all of the unfinished stuff."

"Do not tell me you still love him." Janice huffed from her end of the call. "You were both kids, it was a first crush."

"You're too cynical. You know as well as I do how many high school sweethearts from our class are still together."

"Because they don't know any better. They never left Avery to see what other fish might be in the sea."

"But he has, and he hasn't found anyone else. That must count for something."

"Jordan Phillip Brooks, do not get stars in your eyes. Trey isn't going to change his stripes, at least, not until he retires. The only road open to you is one to Pain Central. I do not want to have my name splashed all over the news for shanking a professional football player."

"So melodramatic, Jannie," Jordan chided her and then sighed. "I know. I know," he said again louder when she groaned. "Whatever future we might have had died at that intersection. We are in two different worlds. I'm just trying to give him some answers and hopefully some closure."

"That may be what you intend, but I know you. You were never able to say no to him."

"And, I'm a grown man. Whatever happens, I'll deal with it."

J.T. Cheyanne

"Sure you will," she grunted. "I'll help put you back together again. Maybe. Depends on what you bring me from Denver. Get out of that room and quit waiting on him. Get out there and do some sightseeing."

"I was on my way out when you called."

"Uh-huh, that's what they all say. Later Jordan."

"Bye-bye, Janice."

Jordan tossed the phone on the bed and slouched down in the chair. He knew Janice only wanted what was best for him. But, she was also the one who had suffered the most when he and Trey had started dating in high school. They had been inseparable before Trey came into the picture and she'd resented Trey for monopolizing his time. Unlike his parents, she encouraged his separation from Trey after the accident. She argued adamantly that Trey should have come back to check on him, and she resolutely refused to forgive him for never showing up.

Wallowing in the past wasn't going to get anything done, and neither was hiding in his hotel room. Janice was right, he needed to do something. Jordan pushed up from the chair and grabbed the phone. After a quick check in the mirror, he headed out.

~*~*~

The faint buzzing of his cell phone pulled Jordan from a fitful sleep. He blinked at the blurry screen trying to make sense of the glowing numbers. His contacts were in the bathroom and his glasses eluded his searching hand. He fumbled to hit the fuzzy green blob on the screen.

"Hello."

"Jordan, hey. What's up?"

"Apparently, you are."

"Yeah, I was heading home. We had a thing after practice that I totally forgot about. I was just wondering if you wanted me to stop by for a nightcap, maybe we could talk some more?"

"What time is it?"

"Quarter to one, I think. No practice tomorrow so the late night won't matter."

Jordan rolled over in bed while he considered his answer. He'd spent the entire evening alone waiting for Trey to call. He'd hurried back from his visits to the LoDo district and 16th Street Mall to stash his purchases and shower. He'd thought about ordering room service, but there had been some really cool jazz bars downtown so he'd decided to wait for Trey.

By ten o'clock, he'd given up and stripped down to boxers and a t-shirt. He'd drifted in and out of sleep with Janice's words swirling in his head. They pushed to the front of his mind. The night was a perfect example of what he didn't want in any type of relationship with Trey. Waiting. Wondering.

"What kind of function was it?" He blurted the question into the silence.

"I can tell you about it when I get there."

"Actually, tell me now. Were spouses invited? Girlfriends?" Silence met his questions. "I'm guessing that means yes. Did it even cross your mind to call and ask me to go?"

"Jordan, I…"

"Don't, Trey. Don't make excuses. I came out here because you asked me to, and I probably deserve being ditched. I mean payback's a bitch right, and it's not like we're dating or anything."

Jordan stopped talking and exhaled slowly. "Look, I don't know what I expected when I came out here. I mean, I knew you'd have practice and the game. We needed to talk and we did that last night." Jordan closed his eyes and massaged his temples. Frustration, and hurt if he was honest, gave him the backbone Janice thought he lacked. "Besides, I'm already in bed. Just go back to your hotel, okay. Whatever we're trying to do, it's just craziness."

"I'm only about ten minutes away. Just call the desk and have them give me a key. You won't even have to get up."

The temptation was there, but he couldn't do it. "No, Trey. It's late, and I'm just not in a good place to have another fight with you. Maybe, I'll see you tomorrow." Fingers shaking, he ended the call and muted the phone. He tossed it to the empty side of the bed and slid back down in the rumpled sheets. When it vibrated, he thought about turning it off completely. If not for his dad's health, he would have.

J.T. Cheyanne

Chapter Sixteen
~ * ~ * ~

Pre-game day dawned bright and clear. Trey knew because he watched the first rays of pink, orange and blue streak the sky behind the mountains. He'd stopped trying Jordan's number after the third trip to voice mail. He hadn't bothered with a message.

At first, he'd been furious that Jordan would hang-up on him. He was supposed to be in Denver so they could talk. After closing himself in his hotel room and re-hashing the brief conversation, he shrugged off the anger to accept the itchy mantle of guilt.

Jordan had basically skipped out on his job, put his life on hold and incurred what had to be major expenses on a teacher's salary because Trey had asked him to come. He'd spent the entire day alone in an unfamiliar city waiting for Trey. Without a second thought, Trey had blown him off to attend a function that, in all fairness, Jordan could have attended with him. Janice's and Jordan's words danced wicked circles in his mind.

Had he expected Jordan to hide in the shadows of his life? What had his expectations been for them? He certainly hadn't considered all of the angles of their relationship and how it would affect both of them. He'd done the same as he always had. He had been a teenager, full of dreams and ideals. He set goals and expected to reach them. He definitely hadn't been realistic where Jordan was concerned. Had Jordan made the right decision after all?

Trey rejected that notion. They would have figured it out. Things might have been different, maybe he wouldn't have made it to the pros, but they would have been together. That had been his most important dream. Not football, not fame, not money. Just Jordan.

So, why hadn't he taken Jordan to the pre-game party?

The question rattled him because the answer cut deep. He was afraid. If he took Jordan, he would have to stand before the world and admit who he really was. What kind of role model was he after all? He chose to hide in the shadows of his personal life. What was that telling the younger generation? What was that telling Jordan?

Trey retreated from the glaring eyes of the sun and the truth. He found the hotel gym and spent two hours running, lifting and cursing. Physical exhaustion finally corralled the twisting thoughts into submission. Back in his room, he climbed into the shower and let the hot water soothe aching muscles. When he fell across the bed naked, he only wanted the oblivion of sleep.

~*~*~

"Hey man, you in your room?"

"Yeah, what's up?"

"I'll be there in a sec."

Trey sat up and scrubbed a hand over his face. The screen said it was two in the afternoon. There were no messages from Jordan. Trey shoved up off the mattress and hit the lights and then the bathroom. A hard knock on the door echoed his flush.

"Hang on," he yelled while digging through his gear for boxers. He also pulled on a Wildcats tee shirt before swinging the door open. Silas gave him a once over and lifted a brow.

"Rough night?"

Trey grunted. "You coming in or what?"

Silas strolled into the room and took the chair by the windows; the one Trey had used most of the night. Trey stretched out across the bed again. He looked at Silas and the decision clicked. It was time to step out of the closet.

"I need to tell you something."

"You got laid last night?"

"Not exactly." He flicked a glance at Silas, who was staring out of the window. "I'm gay."

"Yeah, that was pretty obvious from the lip-lock behind the diner." Silas turned his head so their eyes met. "You're planning to come out?"

"I think I need to." Trey rolled over and scooted up the mattress so he leaned against the wall-mounted headboard. "Jordan's here in Colorado. I asked him to come so we could talk about what happened after high school."

"You dated back then?"

"Secretly. Small town, big gossip and bigger dreams. We were going to leave together when we graduated. I left for college thinking, no believing, he was going to follow. He never showed up." Trey shrugged. "He says he didn't because he thought it was best for me."

"He was probably right." Silas shrugged away Trey's glare. "I'm a damn good agent, and you're a phenomenal athlete. I don't think either would have mattered if you had come out."

"And now?"

"A lot has changed in twenty years. Still, football is a man's sport and most heterosexual males aren't comfortable with a gay man, especially as a role model. That's why most athletes in the league don't come out until after retirement."

"I never aspired to be a role model; I just wanted to play football."

"But, it's part of the job."

J.T. Cheyanne

"Well, then I'm a lousy one." Trey sighed. "What am I saying to all of those gay kids who want to play football, or baseball, or whatever sport they choose? Shouldn't I be telling them it's okay to be who you are? What are they going to do?"

"Mostly, they'll do the same thing you've done. They'll hide it."

"And, that's bullshit. For them and for their future partners."

"I take it Jordan's changed his mind about keeping quiet."

"Not at all. He's determined as hell about that. I've never known him to be so stubborn. He is upset with me. I left him hanging last night and went to the team party." Trey flung himself off the bed and started to pace. "The others had their wives or girlfriends there, and I never even thought to ask him if he wanted to go. He should have been there; he should have always been there."

Trey stopped pacing and stared at Silas. "All of this time, I've been hiding behind my helmet and jersey. What message does that send? What does it say about me?"

"That you did what you had to do to play a game you love."

"That's not good enough." Trey dropped back on the edge of the bed, shoulders slumped. "I've been mad at Jordan for two decades, accusing him of being a coward when in fact, I was the yellow-bellied, scaredy-cat. He's out and lives his life unapologetically, in Avery, no less."

"So, you want to come out now? With your contract hanging in the balance?"

Trey raked both hands through his hair. "I don't know, damn it. I just know I've been up all night trying to figure out what the hell is going on with my life. A month ago, everything was normal. Then you wanted to go to that damn reunion. I saw Jordan, talked to him, and now everything feels off. I can't concentrate, can't sleep."

"You still love him?"

Trey's stomach flipped. A vice closed around his chest. Air escaped but didn't return. He felt dizzy and hot and…excited. It couldn't be that simple, could it?

"It's been twenty freaking years, Si, how the hell could that be possible?" But, with crystal clarity, he knew it was true. He'd never had much interest in dating and deep-sixed anyone that whispered at the possibility of a relationship.

"You don't have to admit it, buddy. I can see it all over your face." Silas rose from the chair and crossed to Trey's side. He dropped a hand on his shoulder and squeezed. "Seems to me, you've got some decisions to make. Whatever you decide, I've got your back."

~ 73 ~

Surprised, Trey looked up. The usual smirk was replaced with a surprisingly serious expression. "We've been through a lot together. You're not just a client and haven't been for a long time. You tell me how you want to do this, and I'll make it happen. But, be sure about him. If he doesn't feel the same way, you're exposing yourself for no reason."

Trey swallowed the ball of emotion clogging his throat. "Thank you. But, I think I need to do this for myself as much as for him."

Silas gave his shoulder one final squeeze before dropping his hand and sauntering toward the door. "Call him. You have the day free, don't spend it locked in this room going over plays and second-guessing yourself." Without looking back, Silas exited the room, softly clicking the door closed behind him.

Chapter Seventeen
~ * ~ * ~

Jordan took one last look around the room and shouldered his computer bag. The clock on the bedside table read three fifteen in the afternoon. Trey hadn't called or come by. The message was pretty clear. He'd walked right into the trap Trey had laid for him. He wanted Jordan to know how it felt. Jordan definitely got the point. Crossing the room, he swung the door open and flushed.

Leaning against the door jamb, Trey slid a glance over the packed suitcase before meeting Jordan's guilty stare. "Going somewhere?"

"Home." Jordan squared his shoulders and lifted his chin. He refused to let his eyes linger on the beautiful physique displayed before him. He couldn't let it distract him from the decision he'd reached in the longest, darkest hours of the morning.

"Without saying goodbye?"

Jordan shrugged. "I was going to call from the airport."

Not.

He could tell from Trey's eyes that he didn't believe the lie either. "I'm sorry."

The quietly spoken apology caught Jordan off guard. He'd expected Trey to be defensive, probably angry. His resolve weakened.

"It's okay."

"No. It's not." Trey straightened. "I honestly didn't think you'd want to go. You hate football talk and there was a lot of it."

Jordan found his backbone again. "It would have been nice to be given the choice."

The smile dropped from Trey's face. Blue fire flamed in his eyes. "So, now you think that's an appropriate argument? You sure as hell weren't receptive when the shoe was on the other foot."

"It's not the same thing." Damn it. He didn't want to sound defensive.

"Bullshit, Jordan. You cannot say that to me. It's still our lives, it's still about us. You do not get to just walk out on me again."

From down the hall, the sound of doors opening reached Jordan's ears. Even without his jersey, Trey was too recognizable. If anyone looked, they would see Jordan. Stepping back, he waved Trey inside.

"Get in here," he snapped in a harsh whisper and quickly closed the door in case anyone had ventured closer. His bag slid off of his shoulder. He let it fall to the carpet. "There is no us, Trey. There hasn't been for a very long time."

J.T. Cheyanne

He turned around to find Trey standing in the middle of the room with his head down and shoulders slumped. The defeated pose was so uncharacteristic Jordan's heart constricted.

"Trey?" When he got no response, he eased closer and laid a hand on Trey's back.

"What's wrong?"

When Trey looked up, the anger had leaked out of his eyes. Sadness and hurt, two emotions Jordan knew well, vied for space. Jordan caught his breath. It tore him apart to see Trey's pain. It had always broken him to see the vibrant and confident Trey brought to his knees by his fear of being found out, of being reviled because he loved another man. It tore his heart out to cause that same look in those beautiful eyes.

In a flash of memory, Jordan saw the teenage boy he'd fallen for so many years ago. He remembered the first tentative kiss. Trey had some experience with girls, Jordan had none at all. Stars had exploded against his eyelids when their lips brushed. Electricity had sizzled along his nerve endings. And then, Trey had wanted more. He'd pulled Jordan into his lap and everything had disappeared except the taste, smell and feel of Trey surrounding him. In that moment, he'd given Trey his heart and soul, and he'd never gotten them back. He saw them there in Trey's eyes. Limp, deflated, but still alive.

Jordan took a reflexive step backward. There was no way he was seeing what he thought he saw. It was his heart playing tricks on him, showing him what he wanted to see. It wasn't possible that Trey still loved him. Not after what he'd done to him, to them. To believe otherwise was delusional.

Jordan grabbed at the unraveling threads of his anger and wound them around his fractured heart. "If you're here to rehash the same argument, you're wasting your time."

Trey's eyes shuttered. Whatever had been in them vanished.

"It's more of an interrogation than an argument. I want answers, and you keep sidestepping the questions."

"I have not. I told you what happened." The very stingiest of details, but it was the truth.

"There's still something you aren't telling me."

"No. There isn't." That was an outright lie.

"Yes, there is." And, leave it to Trey to call him on it.

Jordan turned away and walked to the desk and chair combo along the wall. "Fine, if you must know. I was headed back to Avery when the accident happened."

"That's not what you said before."

Damn it. Jordan twisted around and faced Trey. His voice wasn't steady when he spoke. "I didn't want to hurt you any more than I already had, but you just won't let it go."

Trey studied his face. Jordan struggled not to squirm under his intense scrutiny, but he couldn't hold that harsh gaze.

"You're lying."

Jordan's eyes jumped back to Trey's face. How did he know?

"The tips of your ears go red and you clench your jaw like you're biting back the truth." Trey's smile was tinged with sadness. "That part of you hasn't changed. You never did lie very well. So, I know when you left Avery, you had every intention of coming to be with me. Something awful happened, Jordie. And, I don't understand why you didn't tell me then, or why you keep hiding it now. We were going to conquer the damn world together."

Despite the anger from the day before, despite the warnings ringing in his head, Jordan crossed the space separating them. He hesitated a moment, but the need to stop the suffering in Trey's eyes was too strong.

"Damn you," Jordan stepped into Trey's personal space and lifted his face. "You were the one who was going to conquer the world. I was just along for the ride." He brushed his lips against Trey's chin, stubbly from the night's growth. "You were the brightest star in the sky, Trey. You needed to be free to shine."

"I didn't want to be free. I wanted you."

"I wouldn't have been enough. Not even close." He brought his hands up to Trey's shoulders. "I'm not as strong now as I was then. It was easier when you weren't standing right in front of me. I should resist this, resist you. Walk out the door." Jordan's hand slid up the thick, strong curve of Trey's neck. His fingers tangled in the thick waves of his hair. "But, I can't."

Jordan captured Trey's mouth with his own. Firm lips softened and parted. Jordan's tongue darted in to taste. He moaned, the taste both familiar and thrilling. Trey's big hands grasped Jordan's hips and hauled him against Trey's chest.

Jordan yielded control of the kiss to him. Trey dove in like a starving man. His teeth savaged Jordan's lips and then, his tongue soothed away the sting.

"Trey, God, I need..." and his words were cut off as Trey claimed his mouth again. Jordan relished Trey's aggressiveness; it matched the fire scalding him from the inside out.

"Trey!" A plea. A demand. Jordan didn't know. Everything was consumed with Trey and every point of contact between their straining bodies. The world spun around him. His back slammed into the wall. He barely registered the fierce impact because Trey caught his mouth again and pressed into him pecs to crotch.

Jordan bucked against the hard ridge of Trey's arousal as it seared into his own through their clothes. Trey's big hand slid over his ass and down Jordan's thighs. As easy as picking up a football, he lifted Jordan off of his feet and spread his legs, giving himself a cradle against Jordan's body. Nike track pants and thin khakis did little to cushion Trey's erection. Trey's hips rocked.

Precum leaked from Jordan's diamond-hard cock soaking his boxers. Locking his ankles around Trey's hips, he used the wall as leverage to grind against Trey. The growl of approval from his high school love sent fingers of pleasure along his spine.

He groaned in protest when Trey pulled back. Forcing his eyes open, he almost gasped at the naked hunger on Trey's face.

"Why'd you stop?"

"Your phone's going off." Trey tugged the device out of Jordan's back pocket. He flushed. He hadn't even felt the vibrations. His first instinct was to toss it away, but a quick glance at the screen stalled that notion.

"Mom?"

"Honey, um, where are you?"

"In my hotel room. What's wrong?"

"It's your dad. He fell in the backyard. I don't know what happened. I only turned my back for a second. I don't know if he hit his head. He wasn't responding." His mother's shaky voice conveyed her worst fears.

He needed to go home. He shouldn't have left. Guilt writhed like worms in his gut. Jordan struggled against the confining position. Trey stepped back and held him steady as his feet hit the floor. He did not, however, move away.

"Did you call an ambulance?"

"Yes, they're here now. He's conscious but not coherent. They're worried it may be another stroke. They want to run tests."

"I'm on the way, Mom. Go with him and let me know if anything changes. It's a short flight and my car is at the airport. I'm leaving now. Yes. He's right here. Mom, really?"

Jordan handed the phone to Trey and went to the door to retrieve his bags. Fear wrapped icy fingers around his throat. His dad hadn't fully recovered from the first stroke. The doctors had assured them there were no blockages and his medicine was being carefully regulated. Had his dad forgotten to take it?

The phone appeared in his field of vision. "She apologized for interrupting and made me promise to get you to the airport safely." Jordan reached for the outstretched phone. Trey caught him by the wrist and pulled him into direct contact with his body.

"I don't have time for this, Trey. I need to go."

"I know, and I'm going to keep my promise to your mom and get you to the airport. I have a rental downstairs. But, I want you to know, this isn't over. You're not going back to Avery to hide from me."

"I was never hiding from you or anyone. You've always known where to find me. Can we go now?"

Trey sighed and released him. "After you."

Chapter Eighteen
~ * ~ * ~

In the quiet hours just before midnight, the phone in his pocket vibrated. After a quick glance at his sleeping father, Jordan slipped outside the room and hit the talk button.

"Hey."

"Hey, yourself. How's Mr. B?"

"He's okay. It wasn't another stroke. He stepped in a hole and twisted his ankle. When he fell, he caught the wooden border of the flower garden out back. It knocked him out."

"Damn. Must have been some fall."

"Yeah, he didn't have the reflexes to catch himself so he went down hard."

"Concussion?"

"A mild one. He's a bit nauseated, but otherwise, he seems to be okay. They kept him overnight for observation because of his age and the stroke."

"Mrs. B. okay?"

"Yup, she's at home. I'm sure she'll be back before daylight. She wasn't happy about leaving."

"I'm surprised she did."

"Me too; I had to promise to stay with him every second."

"I should go then so you don't disturb him."

"You don't have to, I stepped outside the room to take the call. Although, you do have a game tomorrow so you should be sleeping yourself."

"It's a late game. I can sleep in. I wanted to make sure you were okay; that your dad was okay."

"He'll be happy to know you checked in on him. He's still your biggest fan."

"I thought that was your title."

All sorts of emotions clogged Jordan's throat at the teasing timbre of Trey's voice. "It was." Jordan cleared his throat. "It is." Geez, he was still such a dork.

"I could use a little fan appreciation." The teasing was gone, replaced by sexy and dangerous. "You left me with a bit of a problem."

"Trey, I am standing in the hallway of a public hospital."

"So, lean against the wall and close your eyes. Picture me in your bed, wearing just my football pants, unlaced…"

Jordan's throat worked, but not a word emerged. Hot blood surged into his groin. In high school, that had been his biggest fantasy. Sweaty, glistening Trey, straight off of the football field in his bed, wearing those tight black and red football pants that emphasized his ass.

"You're quiet. You're remembering aren't you?"

He was. He'd gone to the last home game of the season and sat through four long quarters instead of staying home to study for his Trig test. He'd waited, along with almost all of the female student body, by the field house after the game for a glimpse of Trey, for the quick smile that was for him alone, the wink that meant he would see him later. Except, he never saw Trey come out.

He'd gone home feeling out of sorts and just a bit angry. Trey had never left without some type of acknowledgment. In his bedroom, it had taken him mere seconds to realize why he hadn't seen Trey at the field house. Because Trey was in his bed, front laces undone, one arm up and crooked at the elbow so his head rested on his forearm.

It hadn't been their first time, but it had been one of the best. Trey had given him every one of the fantasies he'd whispered into the phone in the dark with his cheeks burning from his daring. It had been years later before he wondered why his parents hadn't checked on him with all of the thumps and bumps.

"Jordan?"

"I'm here." Breathless, raspy, he barely managed a whisper. There was no way to hide the effects of the memories from Trey. "But, I need to go. The nurse is coming."

"She isn't the only one. Good night, Jordie."

"Yeah." Strangled, voice high, Jordan barely managed to answer. "Good night."

Jordan hung up and leaned against the wall. He attempted a smile for the nurse, the mother of one of his students. The conversation, especially the last part, played through his mind. What was Trey's motive for bringing up that night? Why was he forcing Jordan to remember when it was pretty clear he was still angry about their break-up?

Losing Trey once had been devastating, he wasn't sure he'd survive a second time. Was that Trey's objective? To hurt him, the way Trey had been hurt? He would have to be more careful. No more slip-ups like that afternoon in the hotel room.

He straightened when the nurse came back out of the room. "Your dad is resting just fine. We can keep an eye on him if you want to go home and get some sleep."

Her name flashed into his mind. Jeanine, Everly Sutton's mother, the resemblance was in the eyes. "Thank you, Jeanine, but I promised my mom I would stay with him."

"I can try to get you a rollaway, or at least one of the chairs that converts into a sleeper."

"No, I'll be fine. Hospitals give me the jitters. I wouldn't sleep anyway; someone else may need it."

Her smile fell away. He saw the realization dawn in her stricken eyes. "I'm so sorry. I wasn't thinking."

"It's okay. Like I said, I'm fine." He shrugged away her concern. After the harried flight home worrying about his parents and the unsettling conversation with Trey, he definitely didn't want to discuss his own stints in the hospital. There was only so much a man could handle in one day.

"Mom was so upset; I thought it best she go home and sleep. I have all day tomorrow to catch up."

"If you're sure."

"I am. Thank you." He slid past her into the room. "I'll buzz you guys if we need anything." With relief, he watched her nod and walk away. He closed the door and leaned his forehead against it. His body sagged with the weight of the previous night and the long day.

"You look like you've had a bad day."

Jordan jerked upright. He turned to see his dad awake and watching him. "Not as bad as you. How are you feeling?"

"Slight headache, but okay."

"Your ankle?"

"Not a twinge. I suspect that will change when I try to stand on it."

"You scared us."

His father frowned and patted the bed. Jordan crossed the room and sat on the edge of the mattress. He twined his fingers with his dad's when he took his hand.

"I'm sorry about that. I wish your mother hadn't called you. You needed the time with Trey."

"I would have been ticked off if she hadn't. You're my dad. I want to know if something happens to you." He lifted a shoulder and let it fall, but he knew the gesture didn't fool his pop. "Trey is...probably bored, maybe going through a mid-life crisis. I don't know what he is."

"He's the man you've loved your entire life." With his free hand, his dad reached out and tilted Jordan's head up so their eyes met. "Your mother and I have always supported you. We want you to have a full and happy life the same way we have. We were both so happy when you went to Denver. And then, I go and ruin it."

"Dad, it doesn't matter."

"It does matter, Jordan. It's time you stopped hiding in Avery."

J.T. Cheyanne

Jordan pushed up from the bed and went to the small window. "That's what he said when I was leaving, that I couldn't hide from him anymore." Bracing his hands on the small sill, he looked out into the parking lot just a floor below.

"But, I wasn't hiding. I was right here the whole time. He never came to find me."

"Did you expect him to? You refused to talk to him. You wouldn't let your mother and I talk to him. You cut him off pretty viciously."

Jordan swung around to face his father. The older man held up his hand to stop the response he knew was coming. "All I'm saying is, he didn't know what was going on here. If you'd given him just one spark of hope he would have been here on the next flight."

He couldn't deny his dad's truth. Trey would have left everything, the scholarship, college, his chance at the future he'd always dreamed about. Deep down where it mattered, Jordan knew that. But, Trey had been destined for more than just Jordan and Avery, Wyoming. In the back of his mind, he'd always known he'd lose Trey to the bigger, brighter future. So, he had been ruthless in cutting the ties.

But, would he have been able to let go so easily before the accident? That was the million-dollar question that haunted him. Had he taken the coward's way out? Guilt said yes. His heart said yes. His head, though, the realistic side of him, said no.

Could they have survived the scrutiny of being a young gay couple? Yes, probably, but Trey wouldn't have been drafted. His professional career would be non-existent. Jordan held on to those facts with both fists. There were a lot of days and nights that those facts kept him sane.

"At first, I was terrified he would come back just because I wouldn't talk to him. He was always so clear on what he wanted and he wasn't afraid to go after it. From the moment he decided we were meant to be together, he was a whirlwind. He literally blew me away."

Jordan smiled, but he knew his dad could still see the sadness. "I've never understood what he saw in me. I was the biggest math geek in three counties. Scrawny. Shy. Everything he wasn't."

"He saw your soul, the man you would become. Love does that, Jordan. It hits us out of the blue, and it doesn't care what society says or what it's supposed to be. It just is and it's beautiful."

"And what about the proverb, if you love something let it go."

Danny Brooks sighed. "And you think you're so ordinary. An analytical mind and a romantic's heart. An odd combination in a man. Son, that old saying doesn't place a time limit on the return. You set him free, he's tested his wings and maybe, this is him coming back to you. But, if you want him to stay, you have to tell him the truth."

J.T. Cheyanne

"When he comes back to Avery, I'll be sure and make that a priority."

"You promise?"

Jordan snorted. "You sound like you believe he will."

"I absolutely believe it. Now, promise me you'll stop being stubborn and tell him."

The heart monitor beeped loudly. Alarmed, Jordan closed the distance to the bed. "Fine, dad. I promise." Not like it was going to happen anytime soon. Trey was in the middle of his season. There was talk of the playoffs. Maybe even the Super Bowl.

Jordan fluffed the pillow. "Just lie back and relax, okay. No use getting upset over something that may or may not happen. Thank God, mom's not here or she'd flay me alive."

"I can handle your mother."

"In your dreams, old man. We both know she wears the pants in this family."

"And, she wears them so well."

"Geez, dad. Go to sleep."

Chapter Nineteen
~ * ~ * ~

"Today's win rests solely on the arm of Wildcats quarterback, Trey Bright. He turned in a stellar performance showing up the rookie QB for the Warlords."

Trey hit the mute button on the screen. The win was a plus for him and the team. They were one step closer to the playoffs. Silas would be over the moon considering the ongoing contract negotiations. He knew he should be just as jubilant. Playoffs meant a chance at the Super Bowl, an extension of his contract, more time doing what he loved.

But, all he could think about once he hit the locker room was the one person who wasn't there. For the first time in his life, the win wasn't the most important thing. So, he showered, changed and just walked out. He bypassed the reporters and their cameramen, skipped out on the fans, and even dodged Silas.

No one knew where he was going, except the ticket agent at the airport. He glanced over at the small clock beside the bed. He had to get moving so he could make it through security in time.

Suitcase in hand, he hit the door and drew up short. "Silas."

It was obvious the other man wasn't happy. "You ditched the press." And me. Unspoken but crystal clear.

"Players do it all the time."

"Not the ones with contracts on the line."

"I think the game spoke for me. Four touchdown passes. Two hundred and eighty-six yards passing. We won by two touchdowns against the number one team in the west division."

"Your head wasn't in the game."

Trey stared at him in disbelief. "What?"

"I've watched you play for sixteen years, Trey. In all of that time, you've rarely missed a receiver. There were at least six flubbed passes that were your fault. The receiver was there and the ball wasn't. You could have thrown for twice those yards. You did just enough to get by."

"I don't have to listen to this from you. I did my job. We won. Everyone's happy. Except you. I'm out of here." He pushed past Silas into the hallway.

"You're willing to give all of this up for him?" The shock in those words froze Trey's steps. He swung back to look at Silas. He hadn't really thought about giving anything up, but if it meant he had to stay in the hotel and face a horde of reporters to play the game he loved instead of getting on that airplane, yeah, he was willing to give it up. Jordan called to his soul, a place football had never been able to fill.

J.T. Cheyanne

"Yes." The answer was that simple.

"I wish I could say he doesn't deserve you, but he does." Silas closed the short distance between them and held out a manila envelope. "You wanted answers from him that he wouldn't give you. They're in that envelope. He must have loved you very much. I'm not sure I could have been as strong as he was."

Confused by the sadness he saw on Silas's face, Trey didn't immediately reach for the extended envelope. "Si? What's going on here?"

Silas gave a choked laugh. "You really don't know. I thought you never noticed because of the game and your career, but that wasn't it. It's because you've always been in love with him."

"You aren't making any sense. What was I supposed to notice?" Silas held his gaze. Waiting. Finally, the light bulb went off. Trey's mouth fell open. "Silas, my God, why didn't you ever say anything?"

"Why haven't you?" Silas dropped his head and pinched the bridge of his nose. "Sorry. I know why you haven't. I presented the argument against it only a little while ago. I'm just out of sorts because I find out you are gay, but you're in love with someone else. And, I can't even be mad about it." He thumped the envelope in Trey's hand.

"What's in here?"

"The information you've been trying to pry out of Jordan." Silas looked guilty. "I, ah, might have been a bit jealous after I found you kissing him. I hired a P.I., who by the way, never turned up even a rumor about you being gay. When Jordan said he protected your secret, he wasn't lying."

Trey hated the hurt he saw in his friend's eyes. "This doesn't have to change anything. You're my friend. We'll figure it out. I want us to figure it out, but I have to go now. I've already booked the flight."

"I'll cover for you until Tuesday."

Trey came back down the hall and held his hand out. Silas surprised him by ignoring the hand and stepping in close. Silas's arms circled his waist and for a few moments, Silas rested his head against Trey's chest. When he stepped away, he avoided eye contact.

"Have a safe flight and be careful. Even small towns have reporters."

"We'll talk when I get back. Okay?"

"Yeah, sure." But the agent still refused to meet his eyes. Heart heavy, Trey left him there staring out of the window at the Miami skyline.

Chapter Twenty
~ * ~ * ~

The old Donahue place. Trey's heart thudded in his chest as he looked at it. It had been abandoned for as long as he could remember. Ghost stories about the occupants terrified the neighborhood children. They whizzed past it on their bicycles not daring to look in the windows. Dares and bets were made about spending the night, but if anyone ever had, Trey hadn't heard. Teenagers snuck off together to make out in the dark, eerily silent rooms.

He and Jordan had braved the derelict two-story Colonial on Halloween of their senior year. Instead of fear, Jordan had been enthralled. He wandered through the large rooms, gazed out of the big windows and studied the molding and the fireplaces. In the months that followed, he often talked about the two of them buying the house with the millions Trey would earn playing football, and then restoring it for them to use when they visited their parents.

Trey hadn't thought about the place in years, not since he'd left Avery. But Jordan had bought the damn house and restored it, just like he'd planned. The fact that he had arrowed straight into Trey's heart. Jordan hadn't ever forgotten him. He'd moved into the house they were supposed to live in together. It made believing his story a little bit easier.

Even in the dark, the fresh coat of white paint caught the eye. Black shudders framed the windows on both floors. Gaslights flanked the bright red door, beacons in the night that called Trey to come inside. His eyes lifted to the second floor, skipped two windows to the right. Jordan would be in there asleep. It wasn't the master bedroom, but it was the one Jordan had chosen for them in his detailed fantasies. Trey wondered briefly if the bedroom on the other side of the connecting bathroom was the gym slash office Jordan had envisioned.

Without making a conscious decision to do so, Trey opened the car door, grabbed the manila envelope off of the passenger seat and exited the car. He was halfway up the sidewalk before he paused. It was late, Jordan had classes in the morning. Trey hadn't intended to see him until after school. But, when the address had popped up on Google, he'd had to check it out.

While he debated going back to the car or knocking, a light switched on in the upstairs bedroom. A shadow moved against the curtains. Trey jogged up the sidewalk, took the steps two at a time and knocked.

The door swung open a lot faster than Trey expected. Wearing Wildcats sleep pants and a white undershirt, Jordan shoved his glasses back into place and stared at Trey with a mixture of surprise and wariness.

He ran a hand through his sleep wild hair and cleared his throat. He was the sexiest damn thing Trey had seen in a long time.

"What are you doing here?"

"Checking on you." From the stunned expression, Jordan hadn't expected that response. Good. Trey wanted him off balance. "The last time I was in town, Janice accused me of being selfish. She said I should have come back to check on you. So, here I am. You going to let me in before the neighbors see me?"

"Janice needs to keep her mouth shut," Jordan grumbled but stepped back to give him room. "I'm fine. You shouldn't have come. You must be exhausted after the game."

Trey ignored the brush off. "Your dad okay? I would have called, but figured I should make the effort to be here."

Jordan flushed. "Dad's fine. He went home from the hospital the next day. When I was there Thursday for Thanksgiving dinner, he was chasing mom around the kitchen. Did you see your parents for Thanksgiving?"

"Had the game that day," Trey shrugged.

"Yeah, dad and I watched it."

That did wonderful things to Trey's heart. "We did manage a video chat after it was over and the hotel offering for the team wasn't too bad. I thought about inviting you out, but I know your family does the get together thing on your mom's side."

Jordan continued to stare at him. "I can't believe you're here. You were on the football field only a few hours ago. In Miami."

Trey lifted a brow. "I can't believe you actually bought the old Donahue place."

The flush on Jordan's face deepened. He turned away and headed down the hall. Trey followed him into the kitchen. Jordan flipped on the light, crossed to the side-by-side silver refrigerator and tugged the door open. He pulled out a gallon of milk.

"You want something to drink?"

"No. I had a soda at the airport." Trey studied the granite countertops, the oversized sink and black and white tiled floor. "Looks like you've been here a while. It has the feel of a home, not that spooky feeling like you're being watched."

Jordan slid the milk onto the counter and swung back around. "You didn't come all this way to talk about my house. Why are you here, Trey? What do you want?"

Trey crossed the room and stopped inches away from Jordan. "I want you to tell me why you bought this house." He tossed the envelope onto the counter next to the milk. "And then, I want you to tell me what's in that envelope. I can read it for myself, but I want the truth. From you. Or we'll never have a chance to make this work."

J.T. Cheyanne

Chapter Twenty-One
~ * ~ * ~

Make this work? If not for the counter at his back, Jordan would have fallen over his shock was so great. "Make what work?" Inane question, but that was one of his specialties where Trey was concerned.

"This, us thing," Trey said, waving a hand between their chests. "It's keeping us both awake at night. You've been on my mind all damn week. Janice was right. All those years ago, I should have listened to my heart instead of my coach and come back here to see what the hell was keeping you here. But, I was young and hurt and angry and scared all at the same time. I'm not that kid anymore. My heart and my head told me I needed to be here so this time I listened."

Although the words were exactly what his heart wanted to hear, it wasn't as easy as Trey seemed to think. Jordan was a realist. There was no question that he still loved Trey. It was always there, a part of him as essential as the air he breathed. But, he'd lain in that hotel room in Denver and realized several things about himself. He wasn't willing to live a half-life with Trey. He wanted marriage and commitment, openness. He wanted the world to know Trey belonged to him.

"What about all of the ramifications of "us"? What is your team going to say? Your fans? There's a lot more involved than just the two of us."

"No, there isn't." Trey leaned in, placing his hands on the counter on either side of Jordan's hips. Trapped in Trey's personal space, Jordan resisted the urge to lean forward and rest his head on the broad right shoulder of his throwing arm. He smelled divine and his warmth seeped through the thin cotton of Jordan's t-shirt.

"I have so much I want to say to you, but I need you to be honest with me, Jordie. Tell me why you broke my heart. Why wasn't I enough for you? Why didn't you fight for me? How could you let me go so damn easy?"

The anger was there, but beneath it, the pain vibrated straight into Jordan's heart.

"Don't you know that you were everything to me?" Jordan brought his hand up rubbed his thumb along Trey's jaw. "I lived because of you." Realizing what he'd revealed, he dropped his hand and his eyes. "I bought this house because it reminded me of you, of us. All of those late nights when you humored me listening to my ramblings. It was the only part of "us" that I could have."

The memories were too much, the grief as strong as it had been twenty years before. Jordan pushed out of the cage Trey had made and

~ 90 ~

circled the table. "Even then, I knew you weren't going to live here in Avery. You were so determined to get out and explore the world. You had the talent and the ambition. You're gorgeous and charismatic. It was only a matter of time before you flew out of my arms to live out those dreams."

"All of my dreams, the plans, they all included you."

"I know." Jordan forced a smile. "And, I hugged that close when you were gone. The strength of your love chased away any uncertainty that tried to take root in my head. I never doubted what you felt for me."

"But, it wasn't enough."

"Damn it." Jordan stalked back and snatched up the envelope and then changed his mind. He threw it onto the table and snagged the hem of his t-shirt instead. Taking a deep breath, he met Trey's eyes. "It wasn't about whether you were enough. It was about whether I was." Jordan ripped the thin cotton over his head.

He heard Trey curse, felt the stare as it crawled over the mass of scar tissue stretching from just below his right nipple to down below the hem of his sleep pants. Burn scars from mid-chest around to his spine in places. Ugly, red and in some places painfully twisted. Jordan let him look his fill.

"The accident happened just like I said. I never saw the truck; he didn't have his lights on. The police say he was going about eighty. He slammed into my side of the car. I was trapped. Someone went for help. When the sirens got close, the man panicked. He flicked his cigarette to the side as he ran away. The gas fumes caught."

"Jesus, God, Jordan."

He evaded Trey's hands and his eyes. Crossing the room, he put the table between them and leaned against the wall. "I passed out before they cut me free of the wreckage. When I woke up, I was raw meat full of broken bones. And, I was paralyzed."

"Fuck, this just gets better and better."

Jordan ignored the bitter outburst. If he stopped, he'd never get through the whole story.

"They said it was an incomplete spinal cord injury; the swelling and trauma from the wreck pinched the spinal cord. The actual spinal cord wasn't severed or torn, but my legs were useless. Combined with the second and third-degree burns, the doctors weren't sure if I'd regain the use of my lower body."

"How many times did you flat line?"

The question caught him off guard. He looked up to see Trey's back. The other man's knuckles were white where he gripped the counter. Head bowed and back rigid, he waited for Jordan's answer.

"What?"

J.T. Cheyanne

Trey whirled around, fury spiraling in his eyes. "Do not play stupid with me, Jordan. The evidence is staring me in the face. How many times did you die on that table? How many times did they restart your heart? And, why the fuck didn't someone call me. I loved you. I should have been there at your side."

"You couldn't have done anything."

"I could have been there."

"And lost your scholarship and ruined your chances at a professional career." Jordan bit back that argument. He had to finish the story. "When I finally woke up, I had no idea how long it would take for me to recover, or even if I would recover."

"Would your parents have told me if you died?"

Jordan dropped his gaze to the floor. "Not if they followed my wishes."

The table between them went flying. Trey stalked across the open space, grabbed him by the shoulders and actually shook him once. Jordan didn't object or try to escape because the raw pain in Trey's face robbed him of strength.

Slowly, he lifted his hands and wrapped his fingers around Trey's wrists. Beneath his fingertips, he could feel the furious pounding of Trey's heart.

"I loved you, more than anything. That's why I had to let you go."

"That's the stupidest thing you've ever said." Trey's fingers loosened. He moved to pull back, but Jordan held on to his wrists.

"I knew without a single doubt that you would come back if you found out. My future was uncertain. I wasn't going to ruin yours, too. So, I cut the ties. I refused to let anyone call you and threatened some pretty awful things if they did."

He looked up and read the question in Trey's eyes. "Yes, I threatened to end it. I was in pain. I missed you. I didn't know if I'd ever walk again. It was a pretty dark period in my life. It took a lot of counseling and major rehabilitation to get me on my feet again. I didn't take my first step until two years after the wreck. My muscle tone and coordination were horrible."

"And, when you were on your feet, you still didn't call."

Jordan took a deep breath. This part of the story was the hardest to tell, especially to Trey. "By the time I was walking on my own, I was an addict."

When Trey pulled away, Jordan let him go. "Prescription pain pills," he answered the unasked question. "And when the doctors realized the problem and cut off my prescriptions, I moved on to coke. I spiraled for six years. In and out of rehab. I'd get clean for a few months and something would trigger and I'd be right back to using again."

Jordan bent and picked up the discarded t-shirt. He slipped it over his head before he continued.

"It was always worse during football season. Your name on every station every weekend. Your jerseys in the stores. Every person in Avery following your career. I loved you even then, and I knew that what I had become wasn't worthy of you. The depression would catch up with me and the spiral started all over again."

"I'd like to say I woke up one day and realized I was a dumbass, but I didn't. I overdosed. Janice found me unconscious outside of her apartment. I don't know how I got there or why I was there. I had been living in Jackson, at first because of the rehab, but later it was easier access for my habit. Not a lot of drug dealers in Avery."

Jordan rubbed at the tightness banding his chest. The painful memories haunted him. He pushed past the debilitating emotion. If he stopped, he'd never find the wherewithal to start again.

"It was the terror in my parents' faces that finally reached through the fog. They'd almost lost me a second time. I couldn't do that to them again.

"I stopped using that day. When I got out of the hospital, I signed up for NA. There were countless nights spent on the phone with my sponsor fighting my own body and mind. In ways, drug rehab was harder than learning to walk again. You turn against yourself."

Jordan shook his head refusing to let the past control him. "When the next term started, I enrolled in college. I got my teaching degree, and I've been clean for eleven years. It hasn't been easy. I still struggle with the addiction. There are days I can't move very well, days that the pain is so bad I have to stay in bed."

Jordan fell silent. The only thing left to say, Trey wouldn't believe.

Chapter Twenty-Two
~ * ~ * ~

Silence stretched between them. Trey struggled with Jordan's explanation. While he'd been hurt, then angry and bitter and definitely stubborn, Jordan had been fighting for his life. All of his assumptions were wrong. It was hard to wrap his head around it all.

"I was devastated when you never showed up." Trey upended a chair that had fallen over and sat down. "I missed you so damn much it hurt. I ached for you, Jordie, especially when I was alone in the dark. When the season started, I tried to convince myself I hated you. I told myself so many times that I was better off without you."

"I get it."

He didn't want Jordan's understanding. He banged his fist against his knee and shook his head. "You shouldn't. You really shouldn't. While I was so busy being angry at you, you were near death. I never even considered that. I was hurting and that made me stubborn."

Trey sucked in air. "I should have made more of an effort to find out why you didn't show up. Janice blamed me at the reunion and she was right."

Jordan sighed. "No, she's not. Don't play what-ifs and for God's sake please don't say 'I'm sorry' because I've heard enough of that particular phrase. It's the past, Trey. My past and I've dealt with it. That's why I kept saying there was no point in telling you. I never blamed you for not coming back."

"Well, I certainly blamed you for not showing up." Guilt fueled nausea churned in his gut. Bracing his elbows on his knees, he bent at the waist and dropped his head in his hands. It didn't help. All of the long years apart, he'd blamed Jordan without knowing the facts. With the harsh truth staring him in the face, he realized he owned as much of the blame, if not more.

"The other day I told you I loved you more than football, that you were the only thing that mattered. But, that was a lie."

"Trey, don't. You didn't know."

"And, I didn't try to find out. Sure, I made a few dozen phone calls, but I didn't for one minute consider leaving campus to come back here to Avery."

"I didn't want you, to."

Trey's head snapped up. "Damn it, Jordan, it wasn't about what you wanted. It was about us. It's about what you needed. There's a huge difference there. You needed me, and I wasn't there for you." Trey scrubbed both hands over his face, but the emotional rollercoaster had him by the throat. A lump swelled there as tears gathered in his eyes.

"I've been so mad at you for letting me down when I was the one at fault. Love is supposed to stand the test of time, conquer all. Your reasons for letting it go were purely unselfish."

"That's not altogether true." Jordan's attempt at a smile failed. "After the skin grafts and everything started to heal, I didn't want you to see me. My own reflection horrified me. And, there was the drug addiction. It wasn't pretty."

Trey shook his head. "The scars wouldn't have mattered to me. It was you and you were everything." He didn't bother to wipe away the moisture on his cheeks. "The drug addiction would have never happened. The brutally honest truth is I'm the one who let you go without ever putting up a fight. It was easier to just keep playing football, to hide in the closet and go with the flow. Janice was right on another level. I'm the coward. I failed us. You deserved more from the boy who said he loved you. You still do."

"This is why I didn't want to tell you." Jordan sat down in a chair opposite him. "There is no blame for you to shoulder, and you've never in your life been a coward. It's all in the past. The re-telling hasn't made anything better; it's only shifted the shit-storm around."

"I should've…"

Jordan reached out to rest his fingers against Trey's lips, shushing him. "You were where you needed to be. You've become everything you wanted to be. That's made my life easier, knowing the sacrifice was worth it."

"So, if I hadn't gone pro, you would've called me?"

Jordan dropped his hand and shook his head. "No. I was buried in my addiction by that time. It would have probably caused the depression to intensify. I would have found some way to blame myself."

Trey leaned against the back of the chair. "Did you ever attempt suicide?" The question burned a hole in his gut.

"Thought about it, but never made any actual attempts. I said earlier, I lived because of you, and that's the truth. Even in the darkest hours, there was always this little kernel of light. It was so bright it hurt to look into it because I knew it was you. Your love. I couldn't kill that spark. Not even to make the pain go away."

Trey stared at the man across from him. Strong beyond anything he could comprehend. A survivor. And yet, Trey was the star, the role model to thousands of little boys and teenagers because he played football. At the school, he'd been swarmed by kids Jordan taught every day; kids that apparently had no idea of the struggles their teacher had fought and won.

"I want you to talk to Silas. I want you to be in the documentary thing he's doing."

Jordan jerked to his feet and shook his head almost violently. "Absolutely not. There's no reason anyone has to know anything about me. I never should have told you."

He was in full flight mode. Trey recognized the signs. He caught Jordan at the door to the hallway. "Okay," he soothed. "It's okay. I'm glad you told me. You don't have to talk to anyone. Just breathe, Jordie. I'm right here."

They stood close but only touched where Trey's hands rested lightly on Jordan's hips. Jordan concentrated on breathing; Trey counted each inhale and exhale. Tremors worked their way down Jordan's body. Trey just held him, waiting for the worst of it to pass. Finally, Jordan's muscles relaxed. He lifted his head, eyes haunted by demons Trey had never encountered.

"I have school tomorrow. I need to get some sleep. There's a guest room upstairs. And, a bathroom. You're welcome to stay." But, not in Jordan's bed. The message was clear.

Jordan disengaged and moved to the bottom of the staircase. He looked back over his shoulder. "Let the past go, Trey. Please. I can't go back there again. Tonight, telling you was hard enough." Shoulders sagging, he continued up the stairs and disappeared around a corner.

For long moments, Trey stared up at the grandfather clock at the top of the stairs. Bombarded by his newfound guilt, he struggled to comprehend the enormity of what Jordan had revealed. Paralysis, addiction, depression, suicide. His heart urged him to follow the man he loved, but he owed Jordan his privacy after demanding such a personal confession.

When Jordan's bedroom light clicked off, Trey abandoned his spot in the doorway and returned to the kitchen. The manila envelope lay on the floor, contents scattered. Carefully, he gathered each piece and tucked them back inside. Jordan wouldn't appreciate the reminders. After straightening the rest of the chairs and putting everything back in place, he stretched out on the couch, but couldn't sleep.

His thoughts twisted and turned. Memories of Jordan and their senior year, their love, his college days and the loneliness not quite erased by the success, his career, horrifying images from his imagination of Jordan injured and dying, the wild rush of adrenaline when he'd seen Jordan in the parking lot at the high school, the kisses in the hotel and behind the diner, Jordan's scars.

They had believed they had everything planned, their future set. They'd been so young and so naïve.

Chapter Twenty-Three
~ * ~ * ~

"Don't forget you have detention duties after school."

Jordan forced a smile for the Vice Principal. "Thanks for the reminder, Ms. Garard. I'll be there." When she merely nodded at him, he ducked out of the teacher's lounge and headed for his classroom. He acknowledged greetings from a few students as he wove his way through the milling teenagers waiting for the homeroom bell to ring, but mostly kept his head down.

After going upstairs the night before, he'd tossed and turned for hours. The maelstrom of his memories had stormed his thoughts, finally unleashed by his confession to Trey. Sometime in the early hours just before dawn, he must have drifted off because he hadn't heard Trey leave. When he'd come downstairs just after seven, Trey and the envelope were gone.

In his room, he let the computer bag slide off of his shoulder and propped it against the wall behind his chair. His cup of coffee went on the desk. He dropped into his chair and exhaled harshly. His back was sore and stiff, but not too painful. He'd almost called in, he didn't have the energy to deal with teenagers. But, he'd forced himself to get dressed and make the drive.

It was stupid to be disappointed that Trey hadn't stuck around, even more so, to wallow in self-pity. He was a grown man with a job, obligations. What example would he set for the students if he laid out because things didn't go the way he wanted?

When the bell rang, he made an effort to pull himself together. He pasted on a smile and straightened in his chair. Students trickled in through the door and filled the seats, the same as every morning for the last several years. Announcements came over the intercom. Attendance was recorded; excuses noted. And then, the bell for first period rang. Jordan sank into the routine of a normal day, but Trey was never far from his thoughts.

~*~*~

With a last glance at his watch, Jordan closed the door and locked it. "Everyone should have your assignments for detention. Get your books out and get busy. Anyone not working will get a day added to your detention. No talking. If anyone needs help with something, let me know by raising your hand. Most of you know the drill."

A few groans and mutters preceded the shuffle of papers and books. Jordan took his seat behind the teacher's desk and surveyed the ragtag band of students. Most of them were regulars. Class clowns, talkers, a few wannabe bad boys and girls. There was one surprise in the back. Carter sat in the corner, huddled over his desk writing furiously in an open notebook.

He kept his head down through the entire detention hour. He didn't look up when Jordan unlocked the door and he was still sitting curled around the desk several minutes after the other students had fled their cage. Jordan crossed the room and sat on a desk an aisle over from the teenager.

"Everything okay, Carter?"

When the boy looked up, Jordan bit back a curse. Broken glasses sat crooked on the young man's nose, one lens cracked. They did nothing to conceal the black eye and the inch-long gash along his cheekbone. The injuries explained the detention.

"If he was in here, I could have made sure you were separated. There's a classroom next door you could have used."

Carter shook his head. "Jared didn't get detention because I started the fight."

Jared Hawley, defensive lineman on the football team and goalie for the hockey team. He was a big guy, probably had a good hundred pounds on Carter.

"So, you came to school with a death wish this morning? You need to talk to the counselor?"

"No and no. He should have minded his own business. I wasn't talking to him." The boy's tone was defensive and angry.

"You couldn't have just said that?"

Angry eyes flashed as Carter popped up out of his chair. "Yeah, I could have, but he wouldn't have listened. He'd just laugh like everyone else. 'Look at the gay kid, he's so scrawny, haha. His brain weighs more than his body. Snicker, snicker. And, oh yeah, he thinks Trey Bright would even notice him. How stooooopid.' And, that's just from today. It's nonstop with them. I just want them to shut up and leave me alone."

Jordan's temper flared even as his heart went out to the kid. He'd been there, in those same shoes. He'd never had the courage to fight back. He'd been better at avoiding his bullies.

"He's wrong, you know." Jordan moved around the desk and squeezed into the seat. He waved a hand at the seat behind Carter. "About Trey."

Blinking away tears borne of frustration and anger, Carter sat. "How do you know?"

"Because I was you twenty-one years ago." He easily read the skepticism on the boy's face.

"It's true. I was about a buck thirty, soaking wet. Math nerd." Jordan chuckled. "No surprise there, I bet."

"What's that got to do with Trey Bright?"

"We both went to school right here. Same class. I had a huge crush on him, along with most of the girls in the entire school." Carter's eyes went wide at the admission. It was the first time he'd ever confirmed to a student that he was gay. Jordan continued as if the admission wasn't a huge deal.

"He was gorgeous, charismatic and totally intolerant of bullies. My nemesis was Phillip Parker. He played football with Trey. The summer break before our senior year, Parker decided he was going to toss me in the dumpster behind my parents' diner. Trey stopped him."

"You're lying." Carter shook his head in disbelief. "I mean, I know he went to school here, but why would he stick his neck out against his teammates?"

Jordan debated his answer. He couldn't answer the question truthfully without Trey's consent. Making a snap decision, he pulled his phone out of his pocket. He held up a finger asking Carter to wait. Trey answered on the second ring. He sounded out of breath.

"Hey, I, uh, are you busy?"

"Sort of, but I can take a break. What's up?"

"I have someone here who needs to talk to you. He's a student here at the high school. I'm going to hand him the phone if that's alright?"

"Yeah, sure. Is everything okay?"

"Yup. You, ah, remember how we met before I started tutoring you?"

"Parker?"

"Yeah."

"Put him on the phone."

Jordan extended the phone. "Trey wants to talk to you. You can ask him your question." Carter's face faded to white and then flushed. He stared at the phone.

"You have Trey Bright's phone number?"

Jordan nodded. "He's kind of busy." He extended the phone again. When Carter finally took it, Jordan stood up and walked to the front of the classroom giving the kid some privacy.

It was a risky move calling Trey. Carter would have questions. Jordan couldn't answer all of them without spilling secrets that weren't his alone to share. But, there were far too many stories of gay teens committing suicide on the news for him to ignore Carter's pain. He knew all too well how the lure of the freedom from pain could call so loudly.

Several graded papers later, the phone appeared in his line of vision. "He wants to talk to you before he hangs up."

Jordan accepted the phone and looked up to see stars had replaced the tears in Carter's eyes. He was smiling. Score another save for Trey.

"Thank you, Mr. Brooks."

"Sure thing, and next time Jared is giving you grief, come see me, okay."

"I will."

Jordan watched the young man disappear through the door before he put the phone to his ear.

"Thank you. I kind of got myself in a bind and didn't know what to say."

"Not a problem. I'm glad you called. He seems like a good kid."

"He reminds me of myself back in the day."

"Listen, I'm sorry I skipped out without saying goodbye. I don't want you to think it had anything to do with what you told me."

Which is exactly what he had been thinking all day. Still, he denied it. "I figured you needed to get back to the team."

"I bet if I was there right now, I'd see your ears turning red."

Jordan thanked the Lord Trey couldn't see him through the phone as the flush deepened, heating his skin.

"I have some things to figure out. It could take a few weeks. The end of the season is coming up and it looks like we're going to make the playoffs."

The brush off. He'd known it was going to happen, but it still hurt. "You don't have to explain anything. It's not like we're in a relationship anymore."

"Damn it, Jordie. This is not goodbye."

"Of course it's not." Jordan forced a light note into his voice. "I'm sure the last part of the season will be great. You're the best quarterback in the league."

"I can tell you don't believe me. I'm going to prove you wrong, Jordan Brooks."

"Good luck on Sunday. Dad and I will be cheering you on."

"Jordan!"

"Bye, Trey."

Jordan hung up with Trey's exasperated sigh in his ear. He didn't' hold out much hope in seeing Trey back in Avery except via a television screen. But, one good thing had emerged from Trey's last visit, the call with Carter. Jordan intended to keep closer tabs on the teenager.

Chapter Twenty-Four
~ * ~ * ~

"Trey? What are you doing here?"

"We need to talk."

"Seriously, we don't. Everything's fine."

"No, it's not fine. I owe you an apology or something." Trey shoved his hands in his pockets. "I must have been pretty self-absorbed. I can't believe I never picked up on your feelings."

"It's not like I was shouting anything from the rooftops." After a hearty sigh, Silas stepped back and waved him inside. "I'm guessing you're not leaving until we hash this out."

"You'd be right." Relieved that Silas hadn't slammed the door in his face, Trey stepped inside and kept going down the hall. Familiar with Silas's home, he took the few steps down into the den. He turned to find Silas still at the top of the steps. Wary grey eyes studied him.

"That is exactly why I'm here." Trey lifted his hand to point at Silas's face. "Since when do you look at me like that? We're friends. We've been friends for sixteen damn years."

Silas shrugged one shoulder. "It's not every day a man gets confronted by his crush."

Trey dropped his arm and then raked both hands through his hair. "I'm not here for a confrontation. I just want to talk to you."

"I let you in didn't I?" Silas came down the stairs and went to the corner bar. He fixed himself a gin and tonic before turning back around. "So talk."

"I'm sorry."

"Just stop, okay. Stop right there. You don't owe me an apology or even an explanation. If I'd been braver, I would have told you how I felt. I should have trusted in our friendship and believed that you wouldn't react negatively."

"The world we live in doesn't make it easy to be brave. I hadn't come out either. To you, or to anyone. I wasn't indifferent to the world around me; I was hiding from it." Trey wasn't about to let Silas shoulder all of the blame. He sucked as a friend. He'd been so invested in his own life and his own career, he hadn't paid attention to the person closest to him. Looking back, he realized that other than his parents and his teammates, Silas was the only constant person in his life. Sure, he had friends, but they were all players or trainers. And, none of them knew him as well as Silas.

"When Jordan didn't show up, I nearly lost my scholarship. I couldn't function. So, I locked it all away and focused on the anger. It got me through that first year. But, the anger faded to numbness, and I just didn't allow myself to connect. I didn't see it then, but I can now. I owe you an apology for being a half-assed friend."

Striding over to the couch, Silas dropped down onto the leather cushions. He took another slow sip of his drink before he spoke.

"We can play the blame game all day. It's not going to change anything. You're in love with Jordan. You have been since you were seventeen years old. I can't compete with that. After reading his medical file and the other stuff in that envelope, I don't want to." Silas looked away, took a quick sip of his drink, and then shook his head.

"What?"

"I didn't hire the P.I. on a whim. I did it before we ever left Avery. I wasn't sure what was going on between the two of you, but in all of the time I've known you, I've never seen you react so vehemently about a person.

"The horde of women that swamp you at events, they never garner more than a friendly smile, and to be fair, neither do the men. But, with him, you were fiery, protective, involved. You were ready to toss me out on my ass. I've never seen you so passionate about anything unless you were on the field.

"When I found you kissing him behind the diner, I had to face some hard truths." Silas glanced back at him then. "I planned to fight for you, and then, I read what was in that envelope. He's suffered so much, and so much of it alone because he set you free."

"He didn't have the right to make that choice."

"Yes he did, Trey."

Trey circled the couch and sat down. He knew the anger showed on his face, but before he could speak, Silas held up a hand to stop him.

"I know he hurt you, but you have to look at it from his side of the hospital bed. He was paralyzed facing months, if not years, of recovery. He had no idea if he'd walk again. He knew your ambitions, your dreams. He loved you so much he let you go to chase those dreams. I'm not sure I could ever be that unselfish."

"I didn't come here to talk about him." Trey didn't want to delve into the chaos of his emotions. He just wanted to clear the air with Silas.

The other man gave him a sad smile. "Sweetheart, there's no discussion about your love life that doesn't include him. He's the shadow in your eyes, the part of your smile that keeps it from being complete; he's the part of you that's missing and no one will ever be able to fill those holes except him."

Trey shot up from the sofa and prowled around the room. His thoughts cartwheeled from past to present, from Jordan's explanation to

Silas's words. Strong hands closed over his biceps. Startled, he looked up and met Silas's eyes.

"We're okay. Still friends. I've got your back the same as before." A lopsided smile appeared. "Besides, now I can stop sneaking glimpses of your ass and just openly gawk at it."

Trey barked out a laugh despite the sadness he could still see in Silas's eyes. It was pretty obvious the other man wanted to move ahead. "Funny, I didn't peg you as an ass man."

"Ripe and round my friend, like a juicy tomato."

"You think my ass looks like a tomato?"

"Perfect for a good squeeze and a tasty bite."

Trey laughed again. They were going to be okay. He'd make sure of it. Somehow.

Silas stepped back and dropped his arms. A toothpaste commercial-perfect smile curved his mouth. "Now, let's talk about your man."

Trey's smile faded. "I don't have a man. He's convinced we've outgrown each other. He keeps sending me away."

"He's scared you'll be forced to make a decision. Him or football. He understands the risk you'll be taking if you come out."

"It's my risk to take, dammit. He can't keep making decisions that affect both of us." Trey wasn't about to address the football versus Jordan issue. It tore his heart into shreds knowing that even unconsciously he'd made the wrong choice the first time around.

"So, you are going to come out?"

"I don't know." Trey slouched down onto the sofa again. "It's not anyone's business but my own who I love. Then again, I have this huge platform to tell the world that it's okay to be gay. How can I just hide my head in the sand when there are so many kids who are bullied and tormented every day and teenagers roaming the streets because their parents are assholes?"

He twisted around to stare at Silas. "I talked to one of Jordan's students yesterday. He's my Jordan only twenty years later, being bullied by the jock at school. Nothing's changed in that school except he doesn't have someone like me there to protect him."

"He shouldn't have to be protected, but I get your point." Silas came around and sat on the chair opposite. "I'll support your decision whatever you choose to do. The contracts are signed for both sides. If they void them, you'll still get a sizeable chunk of change, and we still have the endorsements."

"Which would dry up as soon as the contract was shredded and you know it."

"Not necessarily."

"I wouldn't bank on them." Trey shifted forward. "I'm not sure I'm ready to give up football. I love the game. I shouldn't be forced out just because I love a man."

"I agree. You shouldn't, but are you willing to fight that fight? Take on the league and the owners if they void your contract?"

"If that's what it takes, I guess I'll have to be."

"You don't have to make a decision today. Think about it. Talk to Jordan, your parents. Feel out your teammates, see what they think."

"How am I going to do this?"

Silas dropped a hand on his shoulder. "You'll take it one step at a time and the rest of it, that's my job. I'll handle the media, and I think I know what to do. Let's take a look at what I've put together from the visit to Avery."

J.T. Cheyanne

Chapter Twenty-Five
~ * ~ * ~

Trey watched through the large picture window of the dining room as his parents walked hand in hand through the snow. A bright smile curved his mom's mouth. His dad laughed and tugged her closer. He wanted what they shared. A lifetime love. Would they understand his choice?

He rubbed at the ache in his chest. They knew Jordan, of course. His parents owned the only diner in town, and he'd been Trey's tutor. He'd been in their house as much as Trey had been at Jordan's home. But, he'd never told them about the boy he'd had every intention of marrying.

When the front door opened, he strolled out of the dining room to meet them in the hallway. They tumbled inside still laughing and holding on to each other. His mother spotted him first.

"Trey!" She untangled herself from his father and hurried forward to hug him. "We weren't expecting you. You should have called. We could have met you at the airport."

"It was a last-minute decision. I, uh, I need to tell you guys something before it goes viral on the news and internet."

"Are you sick? Injured?" Caroline Bright asked, fear in her voice.

"No mom, I'm fine."

"I knew that boy hit you too hard on Sunday. I told your dad as soon as it happened. I could tell you were shaken up."

"Mom, I promise, I'm fine."

"Come on, Carrie. He said he's okay."

"But…"

"No buts, let's get our coats off and we'll have some coffee in the kitchen. Right, son?"

That was his dad, always the practical one. Allen Bright had taken his father's ailing hardware store and turned it into a thriving multi-state business. His success had been instrumental in proving to Trey that hard work and perseverance paid off.

While they divested themselves of their outerwear, Trey moved down the hall into the kitchen. By the time they joined him, he had three mugs on the counter and coffee dripping into the carafe. No one spoke until they sat around the table.

"I went back to Avery for the class reunion." Trey broke the silence. "I made a donation to the high school. Silas went with me. He filmed a lot of footage; there's going to be a documentary or something on ESPN."

"You didn't fly all the way out here to tell us about a documentary."

J.T. Cheyanne

Trey toyed with his mug, twisting it around and around. His mother reached out and covered his hands.

"You can tell us, baby."

A knot formed in his throat. This was every bit as hard as he'd expected. He let go of the cup and twined his fingers around his mom's hands.

"When I went back, I ran into someone. It made me think about my life."

"You've had a good life. You're living your dream. Not many people get to do that."

Trey shoved up from the table, wincing at his mother's surprised gasp. Why did everyone keep saying that? There was more to life, more to him, than just football.

"I had other dreams, mom. Outside of football." He hated the bitterness in his voice. It wasn't her fault. It wasn't anyone's fault but his own. He met her eyes, saw the confusion in them. He dropped his gaze without looking at his dad.

"Do you remember Jordan?" Just saying his name in front of them robbed him of breath. He was really going to expose his deepest secret.

"He was your math tutor. I believe he's teaching at the high school now. The last time I checked in at the Avery store, Dewey mentioned his boy was in his class."

"He was a nice boy, always polite when he was at the house. Very quiet." His mother added.

Trey braced his hands on the back of the chair he'd just vacated. He stared at the floor and took a deep breath.

"I was in love with him."

Silence.

"He was supposed to meet me at the university when school started." The pain of that day squeezed his chest. Alone in a new place, he hadn't had anyone to confide in, no one to console him. "We were going to get married." The tears came then, ones held in for too many years. He couldn't stop them.

He heard the chair legs scrape across the floor. He braced himself for the questions, the disbelief, and the outrage. He wasn't prepared for the arms that slid around him. His mother pulled him close, smaller than him, but definitely the stronger one at the moment.

"Shh, baby. Mama's got you."

A second set of arms circled him. He felt his father's hand stroke his head. And, he cried harder. For himself, for Jordan, and for all of the time they'd missed together.

The story poured out along with the tears. The sneaking around, the anticipation, the hurt, the anger, and then the reconnection, the accident, the guilt and regret. They held him through all of it, wiping tears, whispering encouragement and above all giving him the support and love he'd known all of his life. It was cathartic and strengthening at the same time.

~*~*~

Later that night, he found himself again at the kitchen table, hands wrapped around another cup of untouched coffee. Sleep eluded him. He couldn't stop thinking about Jordan. He closed his eyes and he saw the scars, remembered the haunted look in the other man's eyes as he talked about the accident. He'd wanted to comfort him, but Jordan hadn't wanted his touch.

A noise on the stairs brought his head up. His father emerged from the night shadows to pause in the doorway.

"You're up late."

"Can't sleep."

"Coffee's not going to help."

Trey glanced down at the still full mug. "I don't even know why I made it. I haven't touched it." Trey pushed the drink away. "I'm sorry if I woke you."

"You didn't." His dad rummaged through the cabinets until he found a bag of cookies. He carried them to the table and sat down. "Your mom's worried about you."

"I'm fine."

"Okay." His dad shrugged one shoulder. He pulled out a cookie and took a bite, offered the package to Trey. He shook his head. "Why did you wait so long to tell us?"

"Come on, dad. You know why. It's all over the news. Parents kicking their children out for being gay."

"It breaks my heart you think we would have done that to you, that we would do that to you." He met Trey's eyes. "You were prepared for that tonight weren't you? To be disowned."

Trey nodded. The words hung in his throat.

"Those parents are fools. The worst thing a parent can ever do is abandon their child." His father took his hand and squeezed. "You are my son. You will always be my son. I don't care who you love. I don't care if you play football or sell used cars. As long as you're happy, that's all I want for you. Nothing and no one can ever take you away from me." His father swiped at the moisture on his cheek. "You hear me boy. Nothing and no one. You don't forget that."

With the last gruff word hanging between them, his dad rose, pressed a kiss to the top of his head and patted his shoulder. At the door, he turned back. "Sitting here thinking about him isn't going to get him back in your life. You've always gone after what you want. Don't let him be any different."

Chapter Twenty-Six
~ * ~ * ~

"Where have you been? Geeezus, the game is about to start."

Jordan tossed his keys on the stand beside the door and grunted when she snatched the casserole dish out of his other hand. "I was helping mom clean up the kitchen and put the food away. Dad had the pre-game on so I haven't missed anything."

"So, you saw the announcement about the documentary?" Janice pushed off the wall and snagged his hand. "You think we'll be on it?"

Jordan allowed himself to be pulled into the living room. He greeted the rest of Janice's ragtag group sprawled all over his furniture. He lifted his chin at Carter who smiled briefly before averting his eyes.

The kid had started hanging out in his classroom before classes began each morning. After the first week, he'd started bringing friends, other kids who weren't in the 'It" crowd. They talked, did homework, ate breakfast, which wasn't technically allowed in classrooms, but Jordan wasn't about to kick any of them out. If his classroom was a safe place for them, he intended to keep it that way even if it meant head-butting with the principal or janitor.

"Considering we avoided the camera, at least I did, and that it's only a preview, don't get your hopes up." He cast a quick eye over the snacks spread out over the coffee table. "Looks like you made yourself at home."

Janice shrugged. "Everyone pitched in. We raided your kitchen for the dishes. Is this the rest of your mom's blueberry cobbler? I think I spotted ice cream in the freezer."

"It is indeed." He turned back to the stairs. "You might want to stick it in the oven and let it heat up. I'm going to run up and shower. I moved some stuff out to the garage for mom and got a little sweaty."

Janice pegged him with a hard stare.

"I'm coming back downstairs. Promise. You can make me a plate, I'll definitely be back for that."

Upstairs, he closed his bedroom door and leaned against the barrier between him and the world. Yes. He'd seen the announcement about the documentary. It was the main reason he'd left his parent's house and come home. He didn't want to watch it with anyone watching him. He'd forgotten about Janice's impromptu Christmas party. But only Janice knew about his history with Trey. Since she wasn't a Trey fan, he wouldn't have to suffer the furtive glances his parents would have tried and failed to hide.

Pushing away from the wood, he trudged across the room. He knew Janice meant well. Sometimes though, a body just needed to be alone. He

J.T. Cheyanne

had no idea what was going to be in the documentary other than the reunion and check presentation. Trey hadn't called and he certainly hadn't been back to Avery. Granted, it was the holiday season and his season was winding down. The last game wasn't until after Christmas.

He needed to stop with the pity party. He'd let Trey go to do exactly what he was doing, live his dream. Tugging the sweatshirt over his head, he tossed it at the hamper. The matching pants followed. He showered quickly, dressed and headed back downstairs.

"Touchdown!" Groans from his living room followed the announcement. Must have been the other team. Jordan slipped into the room and found a spot beside Janice. She handed him a plate.

"You smell good."

"Showers do that." He hefted the full plate. "Thanks."

"Welcome." She shifted around until she leaned against his side. He balanced his plate on his lap. Wings, chips, a cookie, some kind of meat and cheese roll-ups. He chose one of those and took a bite. Pretty good.

While he chewed, his attention shifted to the television. He easily spied Trey in the huddle of men on the field, number fourteen emblazoned on his back. Bright, spelled out in all caps marched across those broad shoulders.

Unbidden, his high school fantasies teased his consciousness. He'd never worn that jersey. Would it feel the same? Would it still hang to his knees despite the changes age had brought with it? Would it smell like Trey?

More memories pushed forward blocking out the game on the television. Trey sprawled on his own bed after football practice, the laces of his football pants undone. The pads were still in place making his thighs look even thicker than usual. The hip pads jutted out low on each hip, the white protective pads even brighter against Trey's sun-darkened skin.

He was bare-chested. Jordan wore his jersey and nothing else. Trey's famous throwing hand lay low on his belly and as Jordan watched it slid south, under the loose strings. They were supposed to be studying, but Trey couldn't focus, or so he said. Trey's hand moved. Jordan's breath caught. A blush stained his cheeks.

"Touchdown!"

Shocked out of his reverie, Jordan jumped, spilled his plate and blinked rapidly. Carter and the others were on their feet dancing in place. On the screen, the footage went to replay. Trey dropped back and shot a bullet from mid-field to the end zone. It screamed past two defenders to nail the receiver in the numbers. Switch back to real-time, the camera focused on Trey jogging to the sidelines, triumphant.

"He has a nice ass."

Trey's gaze swung to Janice. "What?"

"Oh, don't pretend you weren't looking. He has a nice ass. Those pants definitely do him justice."

The comment, so close to what he'd been remembering, dredged up a blush. Janice grinned. Jordan curled his lip at her and leaned closer. "I happen to know it's not the pants at all. It's just as damn nice outside of those pants."

"TMI, my friend, T freaking MI." She said, but she laughed. "You made a mess."

"Yeah, yeah. I'll get it."

After picking up the fallen wings and chips, he slid off of the couch and went into the kitchen. He dumped the plate and food in the trash and sidestepped to the sink to wash his hands.

"You two dated, didn't you?" Jordan swung around to see Carter standing at the door, hands tucked in his pockets. "That's why you have his number."

Jordan dried his hands on a dishtowel as he considered his answer. He didn't want to lie to the kid, but he'd never told anyone about Trey except his parents and Janice. He glanced over Carter's shoulder at the group gathered in the living room.

"Let's step outside for a sec. Grab your coat. It's freezing."

On the back deck, Carter wandered around the perimeter while Jordan struggled with an explanation.

"I won't tell anyone anything you say. I promise." Carter shrugged a skinny shoulder. "I just need something to hold on to you know, when it gets lonely."

Jordan leaned against the railing. "What makes you think we dated?"

"You have his cell number. The way your eyes change when you talk about him. And, the school yearbooks. I went to the library and got all of the ones when you were in high school. There's a lot of jock pictures of him, but not a lot of you. Until senior year. You were on the sidelines for the football team, the basketball team and the baseball team. You managed their stats. In the game photos, you're in some of the background shots. And then, there's this one."

Carter extended a folded sheet of paper. "I made a copy."

Jordan took the folded square and opened it. His heart punched against his ribs. He remembered the exact moment the picture was taken. The football team had won the championship for the second year in a row. The fans stormed the field after the game. It had been chaos. Trey had found him in the crowd. The hug had nearly crushed his ribs.

J.T. Cheyanne

He remembered vividly the hard plastic of the shoulder pads cutting into his chest and shoulders, Trey's strong arms around his waist as he was lifted up off of his feet and over Trey's head. In the picture, he was staring down at a grinning Trey. The crowd celebrated around them.

Not shown in the picture, the look in Trey's eyes. Pure happiness and a love that radiated for Jordan alone. He'd so badly wanted to kiss him right then, right there in front of everyone. The inside of his jaw had been sore for a week afterward from the harsh bite on the tender flesh. Would things have been different if he had kissed Trey that night?

He handed the picture back to Carter. "I have the original upstairs. I stole it from the yearbook photo stash."

"There were a lot of people there. He could have chosen anyone, but he chose you. Because the two of you were together, dating, probably secretly since no one here has ever mentioned it."

"You got all of that from a picture?"

"It's in the body language. He's holding you up, but not away. His arms are bent, keeping you close to him."

"Could be just the way the picture was taken, or he was tired. It was a long game. Brutal as I remember it."

"Doesn't it bother you to deny it? Weren't you proud to be his boyfriend? I would be."

Okay, the time for sidestepping was over. Jordan looked over at the kid and gave him a sad smile. "You're right about the picture. If you notice, I'm not smiling. I'm biting the inside of my jaw so hard it bled. I wanted so very much to kiss him right then at that moment in front of everyone. I wanted them to know he was my boyfriend. Mine. I wanted them to know how proud I was of him. I wanted them to know that I alone shared his secrets and his dreams and that the beautiful boy they all worshiped and loved was going to be my partner, my husband in every way that mattered, just as soon as we could get away from Avery."

Damn, it felt good to say all of that out loud. Carter blinked in surprise. "Then why didn't you?"

Sadness ghosted across his heart. "Because I loved him more than anything in the world and he wasn't ready for the attention it would bring. He wanted to play football, professionally. He wanted to get out of Avery. It's all he talked about. He was never going to do that with a boyfriend hanging around his neck."

"He just left you here?" Jordan saw the betrayal dawn on Carter's face. Like many boys Carter's age, Trey was his hero.

"No," Jordan denied emphatically. Some, but not all of the clouds cleared from Carter's eyes. "Well, he did leave me here, yes, but I was supposed to follow him. It's a very long story that he and I are only just beginning to talk about. But, it wasn't his fault. None of it was his fault."

Janice popped open the back door and poked her head out. "What the hell are you two doing out here; you're missing the game."

"He had a question about a school project. Give us a minute okay."

"That had to be discussed in freezing temperatures, you could have talked inside."

"Janice."

"Fine, whatever." She ducked back inside.

"Carter, I need you to promise you won't tell anyone what we just talked about. I'm trusting you and Trey will be too. If this were to ever come out, he could lose his place with the team. I don't ever want to be the cause of that."

Carter nodded. "I won't tell anyone about him, but, can I still talk to you? About things?" Carter shrugged one bony shoulder. "I haven't told my dad and it gets really hard to cope sometimes."

Jordan went down on one knee in front of the kid. "You can always talk to me, day or night."

"Thanks, Mr. Brooks."

Jordan watched the teenager slip back inside before rising to his feet. It was hard enough navigating high school without having to deal with a part of yourself no one else understood. He hoped Carter gained something from their conversation.

Chapter Twenty-Seven
~ * ~ * ~

Trey watched the promo trailer for the documentary fade to black on the television screen. There were no major reveals. There were some teases about the reunion and his trip back to Avery. Silas had included some of his old high school and college game footage, there were some questions from Silas himself that were asked onscreen, but not answered. And, there were photos from the yearbooks and college programs.

"You ready to face the press?"

"Yeah, sure." Trey stood and took a deep breath.

At the door, Silas stopped him. "You don't have to answer any questions about the documentary. Tell them they'll see it all in a few weeks. Keep it focused on the game. That's the reason they are supposed to be here."

"Come on, Si, it's the press. You know how they can be."

"I haven't heard back from Stromley, yet."

Harlin Stromley, the team owner. Trey's stomach twisted. Was that good or bad?

"He's watched the whole thing?" Silas nodded. "How about I just send you out there?"

"No way, buddy. I can't answer the burning questions about how it feels to know you're only a few games away from the Super Bowl, or why did Brownfield drop that pass on the twenty-yard line when it would have sealed the win early on."

"Press conferences and media types are supposed to be your thing." Trey laughed at Silas's disgusted look and started down the hall.

"That's the downside of the job."

"And the upside?"

"The smoking hot athletes in tight pants, of course." Silas gave him a raised eyebrow look. "Definitely outweighs the media thing.

Trey laughed. "You, my friend, are too much."

They entered the press area to a sea of microphones, questions and flashing cameras. Trey waved at the crowd and worked his way to the table at the front of the room. As he took his seat, he saw Silas standing against the back wall for moral support should he need it.

"Evening everyone, thanks for waiting."

The questions came quick and fast after that. Most of them revolved around the game. Trey could answer those by rote. The last question of the night nailed the elephant in the room.

"We all saw the preview for the documentary. The way it was laid out seems to point to some kind of reveal. We all know you'll be a free

J.T. Cheyanne

agent at the end of the year. Are you retiring? Changing teams? Getting married?" A few chuckles peppered the air. His single status was always fodder in the media. "Is there anything you can tell us at this point?"

Trey pushed up from his chair and smiled at the expectant group. "Afraid I can't spill any beans for you guys. Have a great night and Merry Christmas." He circled the table and headed to meet Silas at the back of the room. A few questions followed him, but he ignored them.

"That went well."

"Yeah, they stayed focused on the game. I don't think I'd have been as lucky if it was earlier in the season. "

"Want to grab a drink?"

"Sure, as long as you don't mind if I call Jordan on the way."

"Fine, but my agreement does not include any cutesy talk. You start that shit, I'm putting you out on the curb."

Trey winked at his agent as he plugged the phone to his ear. It rang twice.

"Hello."

Jordan's husky voice triggered all kinds of reactions in Trey. He wanted to crawl through the phone and into the other man's arms. He wanted to laugh and act the fool and participate in some of that cutesy talk Silas had vetoed. He wanted to be there with Jordan, or have Jordan with him instead of on the other end of a phone. He wanted to touch and taste and feel.

"Hey, you."

Silas rolled his eyes and shook his head. Trey flipped him the finger and pressed the phone tighter to his ear. Other voices carried through the speaker. "You having a party?"

"No, well yes. There are people here, but I didn't, that is, Janice invited the crew over to watch the game and have a pre-Christmas get together. Congratulations, by the way. Great win."

"You watched it?"

"That was the point of everyone being here." Talk about a pinprick to the ego.

"You sound about as enthusiastic as always."

Jordan must have picked up on his disquiet. His voice dropped to a notch above a whisper. "You know I only watch the games so I can see you in those tight pants."

The admission eased the sting. Trey grinned. It wasn't the first time Jordan had told him that same thing. "You're still ogling my ass are you?"

"It's the best one in the league."

J.T. Cheyanne

The compliment came in stereo, from Jordan on the phone and from Silas behind him. "You ready?" Silas mouthed. Trey nodded and followed him outside to the car.

"So how's life in Avery?"

"You know nothing ever changes here. It's the same thing every day."

You could always come and live with me. Trey bit his tongue to stop the words from coming out.

"Carter says to tell you hello."

"He's there?"

"Yeah, he's part of Janice's gang of misfits, same as me. She collects us like rescue animals and keeps us all under her wing. She really needs a houseful of kids."

"There's a soft side under all the teeth and claws?"

Jordan laughed and Trey found himself smiling like a fool.

"I'm surprised you called."

"I told you I would."

"You said you were coming back."

The slight accusation in Jordan's voice widened the grin on Trey's face. "I haven't had a chance. We've been on the road. The season's almost over so it won't be long. I could always send you tickets for another game?"

"You don't have to do that," Jordan protested. "I can't afford another plane ticket so soon."

"I can."

Jordan cleared his throat and changed the subject. "I should probably tell you that Carter asked me if we dated in high school."

Trey waited for the panic to well up, but…it didn't. The world didn't stop. No blaring sirens went off. Just Jordan breathing quietly into his ear through the phone.

"I hope that you told him the truth."

"You do?" It didn't take a genius to mark the surprise in Jordan's voice.

"Yeah. I read the stats about gay teen suicide. He sounded like a really great kid. I wouldn't want anything to happen to him."

"I don't know what to say. I figured you'd be upset."

"I've been thinking about what you said, about our past. And, what I want for our future." Trey felt Silas's gaze on him in the close confines of the car. "I know you don't think we have a future, but you're wrong. I want you to give us a chance again."

Long seconds passed with no response. Trey wished he could see Jordan's face, to know what was going through his analytical, sometimes too logical mind. The eyes always gave him away. And, the ears if he was lying.

"I want to, Trey. I want to believe it's possible, but there's so much at stake for you."

"Stop right there. I don't want you thinking about the consequences or what might or might not happen with my career. Right here, right now, I'm choosing you."

"And, if things don't work out and you're not able to play…"

"Jordan!" Trey interrupted. "Yes or no, just like in elementary school. That's all I need from you right now."

"Yes." The word was so soft, he almost missed it. It didn't help that Silas's stifled laughter filled the car. He glared at the other man before turning to look out the window.

"Jordie?"

"Yes." Much firmer that time. Trey grinned. He couldn't stop it if he'd tried. The tightness in his chest floated away. He saw his grin reflected in the window glass and smiled all the more.

"Then I'm definitely arranging a flight and tickets for the next game. I want to see you at Christmas."

"Trey," Jordan started to object and stopped. "I shouldn't do this, but I can't stop thinking about you. School's closed as of today. I don't have to be back until January sixth. I need to spend Christmas Eve with my parents. I can fly out that night."

"Okay. Yes. I get that." Trey's mind was already racing with plans. He needed to get a tree, arrange dinner and get a gift. "I can't wait to see you."

"I feel the same way. I'll text you my information for the ticket." Jordan went silent for a few heartbeats. "I hope you're serious, Trey. I don't want a relationship in the shadows. I want to stand beside you and tell the world you're mine."

Before Trey could respond, Jordan disconnected the call.

J.T. Cheyanne

Chapter Twenty-Eight
~ * ~ * ~

"Hi, I'm, ummmm, I'm Jordan Brooks."

The man holding the placard bearing his name immediately disappeared the sign and reached for Jordan's suitcase. "I'll take that. If you'll follow me please, the car is parked outside." Given little choice as the man took off with his luggage, Jordan hurried through the busy baggage claim area and emerged into the sunshine.

"Here we are, I'll get the door as soon as I stow your case."

Jordan stumbled to a stop. The limousine stretched long, glossy and black along the curb. "That's for me?" He hated that his voice rose two notches, but the driver didn't seem to care. He merely nodded as he clicked the trunk closed and hurried around to hold the car door open.

"I'm sorry you're having to work on Christmas."

"It's a short trip, sir and Mr. Bright is compensating me well. My family will be waiting when I'm done." He smiled briefly. "The bar is stocked if you wish refreshment. We have Sirius radio for your listening pleasure. The heating and air controls are in the middle console if you become uncomfortable. We have a few hours' drive, not accounting for traffic. Please relax and enjoy yourself."

"Thank you." Jordan slipped into the back of the limo. The leather seats were smooth as silk against his palms. He found the middle console and discovered it controlled far more than just the air. He played with the lights, the radio and the air before the bar caught his eye. He moved forward to inspect the offerings. Soda, water, juice and hard liquor. His gaze shifted left and spied the mini-fridge. He opened it to reveal ice, yogurt, fruit, a selection of deli sandwiches, and eggnog as a nod to the holiday season.

Jordan slid back against the seat and stared in wonder at the luxury around him. In a car. Trey was so far outside of his league it was laughable. What did he know about chauffeurs and limos and multiple homes? There wasn't much room for extravagance on a teacher's salary. The settlement from the wreck had paid for his education and his house. His car, bought used, was five years old.

Jordan shoved the doubts out of his mind. He was on his way to Trey. They were going to share a nice holiday weekend as a couple, with the exception of one very important football game. He wasn't going to let his own anxiety cock-block his time with Trey. Not that he was expecting sex. A flush traversed his body. Okay, that was a lie. Every time he closed his eyes, he pictured Trey in those muscle hugging, ass contouring football pants.

J.T. Cheyanne

And, he had to think about something else. He couldn't show up with a boner tenting his jeans. Frantic for distraction, he yanked his laptop case onto the seat beside him. Inside, a folder overflowed with mid-term tests that needed to be graded. Pulling out every student's worst nightmare, the red pen, he got to work.

~*~*~

Trey bit back a frustrated sigh and moved away from the window. The curtain swished back into place blocking out the winter white surrounding the cabin. His parents had departed early that morning for the warmer temps in south Florida. They had invited him to join them, but he had other plans.

He checked his watch. The flight had arrived on time, but even with the best of traffic, it was still too early for Jordan. So, he paced jumping at every noise outside to check the driveway.

It wasn't the best of times to start a relationship. The playoffs were just around the corner. The stakes were high. When he wasn't on the field for practice, he was in the film room with his coaches. Speculation about the documentary rippled through the sporting world and combined with the bid for the Super Bowl, the media hounded him in and out of the locker room.

He sighed and headed back to the window. Other than the shoveled driveway, nothing marred the beautiful white landscape. His phone rang. He fumbled it out of his pocket.

"Jordan?"

"And Merry Christmas to you, too." Silas. Of course. "I take it he hasn't arrived yet."

"I wouldn't have answered if he had, and Merry Christmas."

Silas chuckled. "I take it you're well-stocked on lube and condoms."

"And, I know that's exactly why you called." Trey shot back. "What's wrong?"

"Nothing, except the star quarterback has ditched his team for a piece of ass."

"What the actual fuck?" Trey roared. "Jordan is not a piece of ass."

"I'm just telling you what's being bandied about and what's likely to appear in the headlines. A couple of your teammates aren't happy with your disappearing act. So far, nothing's been said about it being a him, but you know how things leak. If you don't want his face plastered all over ESPN and Sports Illustrated, I'd stay inside and keep the drapes closed."

"I'm done with hiding, Silas. I told you that. You were supposed to clear it all with the owners."

J.T. Cheyanne

"You were supposed to wait until after the season, or the Super Bowl, whichever came last. If you don't have your ass in Pittsburg for Saturday morning practice, well, I'm not sure what's going to happen."

Trey rubbed at his suddenly pounding temples. Silas was right, as always. He'd spoken to the owners about the documentary. They knew he was coming out. They had sworn they would back him one hundred percent if he waited until after the Super Bowl if they made it that far. If word leaked before, they were well within their rights to boot him from the roster. Not every kid in America got to play professional football. The ones who actually got a contract were expected to deliver on the talent they were being well compensated to display. Practices were mandatory, teamwork required.

"Are they threatening to void the contract?"

"They haven't actually said those words, but if you lose this game, I'd say you can count on it being shredded. They'll use this against you. It's pretty clear your head's not where it needs to be for a Super Bowl bid."

"Would they feel the same if it was a woman?" Trey couldn't keep the anger from his voice.

"They're going to say yes. This is their money maker. Football is their business. You're the star and a bankroll. If you cause them to lose money; you'll be out on your ass and any court in the world is going to side in their favor."

"I'll be there. I'll figure out how to explain it to Jordan." Trey paced back to the window to see the sleek limousine pulling down the drive. Emmanuel, the chauffeur, popped out of the driver's side and hustled around to open the door.

"I have to go, Si. Jordan's car just pulled up. Tell them I'll be there." They exchanged goodbyes. Trey shoved the cell phone into his back pocket and hurried down the hall to the entryway. He waited at the top of the steps as Jordan emerged from the limo.

The other man looked around at the snow-covered landscape and then up at Trey. An uncertain smile tugged at the corners of Jordan's mouth but didn't quite reach his eyes. Trey waited, his own smile so wide his cheeks hurt. Finally, Jordan unplanted his feet and started up the steps.

"Merry Christmas."

"Merry Christmas! I can't believe you're here," he said when Jordan stopped about an arm's length away. He wanted to close the distance and slide his arms around Jordan, feel the sparks as their bodies came into contact, steal a kiss. But, Silas's warning was too fresh.

"Me either. I wasn't expecting…" Jordan turned around and waved at the limo. "It's a bit overwhelming."

J.T. Cheyanne

Trey's grin turned sheepish. "I just wanted to spoil you a little. I know you were planning to rent a car, but this way you got a chance to relax."

"And grade papers." Jordan patted his laptop bag. "Now, I don't have to worry about them while I'm here. I'm all yours."

"I like the sound of that. Come on." Trey gave in to his need to touch and slung an arm around Jordan's shoulders. Casual and friendly to anyone who might be out there. He hated the need to hide, but it wouldn't be for much longer.

Inside the cottage, he dropped his hand to Jordan's lower back and steered him into the small library slash den. As Jordan exclaimed over the ten-foot Christmas tree, Trey stepped into his personal space and framed Jordan's face with his hands. The kiss was soft, tentative and fueled the hunger already brewing in Trey's blood.

He pulled back and groaned when Jordan followed, lips seeking more. Strong hands caught at Trey's hips and pulled him back into the other man's body. The kiss quickly escalated. Jordan's tongue invaded Trey's mouth and he opened wider for the other man. A dull thud bounced around the room when the laptop bag was shrugged off. Geezus, Jordan was throwing off sparks like a firecracker. Trey burned right along with him.

With a strangled laugh, Jordan pulled away and retreated a few steps. An unsteady hand swiped through his hair. "That wasn't...I shouldn't have..."

"If you're going to say, you shouldn't have kissed me, I'm going to strenuously object. In fact, you should definitely still be kissing me with a lot fewer clothes on."

"We need to talk before we do...that." Jordan's cheeks flushed.

"We're going to talk. Before if you prefer, after and hopefully during. I want to know what you like and don't like." Trey shoved his hands in the pockets of his track pants. "You used to be very verbal. I hope you still are."

Jordan shot him a heated look. "We can't base whatever this is going to be on sex. We need a foundation."

"We have a foundation. It just needs a little bit of shoring up. The cracks are there, we both see them, but we can fix it." Trey paused a moment. "If you want to fix them."

"I'm here, aren't I?" Jordan bent to retrieve the laptop bag. "I'm sorry. That's being evasive." He looked directly at Trey. "I want you. I want us. It's all I've ever wanted."

J.T. Cheyanne

"If you felt that way, I still can't understand why you ended it?" Trey couldn't keep the hurt or the anger from his voice. "We could have figured it all out together. Instead, you blocked me out."

The laptop case hit the floor again. The thing was taking a beating. Hopefully, it had some kind of padding, or Jordan would be buying a new one. Jordan paced around the room before falling into one of the leather love seats. Elbows on knees, head in hands, he addressed the floor.

"It was the hardest thing I ever did in my life. Letting you go hurt worse than the burns, or rehab. Mom tells me that every time I surfaced from the heavy meds, I called for you. She nearly broke down and called you so many times."

"She should have." Trey took a seat across from Jordan. "I should have been with you."

"I wanted you there. I wrestled with my own decisions the nights the pain was the worse. I've often wondered if I would have become an addict if I had called you. But, that's irrelevant, isn't it? What's done is gone and can't be changed."

"You were always so focused. I can't imagine you using."

"I was focused until I fell in love with you." Jordan's self-deprecating smile preceded a violent shake of his head. "I'm not saying any of this was your fault. I cherish that year we spent together. The memories got me through withdrawals. But, when I didn't have you to lean on, I found out I wasn't as strong mentally and emotionally as I thought I was.

"Your love gave me the courage to step outside of my comfort zones. Your confidence gave me confidence. When it was all ripped away, I stumbled. Rather badly."

"Why didn't you ever just pick up the phone?"

"And tell you what?" Jordan's shame-filled eyes broke Trey's heart. He switched sofas and sat down as close to Jordan as he could.

"That you made a mistake. That you wanted to talk."

"I never intended to tell you any of this."

Jordan's bare honesty didn't surprise him so much as it saddened him.

"It wasn't because I thought you'd reject me. In fact, it was the opposite. Like I told you before, I knew if you found out you'd leave school and come back to Avery. I didn't want you to risk your scholarship. I really believed I was making the right decision. When you were drafted, it reinforced that belief. You were where you needed to be.

"At the same time, it killed me that you apparently didn't need me. When I was sober, I knew that was unfair. I hadn't given you much choice. It wasn't a pretty time in my life, Trey. I was strung out, living one high to the next. If you had come back then, the shame may have killed me. I knew what I was doing was stupid, but the cravings were so strong and when I was blissed out, I didn't hurt."

Jordan shot up from the sofa, his agitation visible in the shaking hands and restless pacing. At the window again, he reached up and shoved his glasses back up on his nose. The angle of the sun beyond the glass highlighted Jordan's profile. Memories of their past flooded him. In that moment, Trey knew. Football didn't matter, the endorsements didn't matter. The long years of separation didn't matter.

Nothing mattered.

Except Jordan.

Chapter Twenty-Nine
~ * ~ * ~

Nothing outside of the window registered. Every one of his senses was tuned to the man sitting on the sofa. He wanted, with all of his being, to have the future they had always planned together. But, could Trey forgive him? Could he accept Jordan, scarred on the inside and outside? Was he willing to give up one love for another?

Jordan froze when Trey finally rose slowly from the couch. From his peripheral vision, he watched the other man come closer. A big hand rose to gently pull Jordan's glasses free. Jordan's heart stuttered against his ribs.

"That makes twenty times, by my count." Low and demanding, Trey's voice skated over Jordan's skin. "You know what comes next."

He did. Jordan lifted his gaze to find Trey's eyes locked on his mouth. The leg of Jordan's glasses bumped against Trey's lush lips. One eyebrow rose in question. Even as he tilted his head, his lips parted, hungry for the taste of Trey's kiss. The slightest brush glossed over Jordan's parted lips. The moan of disappointment drew a chuckle from Trey.

"Eager are you?"

"Yes." He had no shame. Even with the papers to grade, he'd spent most of his journey in the limo thinking about Trey and the time they were going to have alone. Despite his best efforts, those thoughts had ventured into the erotic.

Smiling, Trey took a step back. And then, another. With a little growl of frustration, Jordan followed, much to Trey's delight if the spreading grin was any indication.

"I intended to have dinner first, maybe a walk around the property. Sex wasn't on the agenda, but if that's what you want, I definitely want to be a good host."

Jordan faltered. Insecurity dropped around him like a wet blanket. Was he wrong about Trey? About what the weekend away meant? Before the doubts could find a foundation, Trey was there. The second kiss was not so chaste. Trey swept him up in an embrace that lifted his feet from the ground. His tongue demanded and gained entrance, plundering and tasting until every bone in Jordan's body went lax. Trey supported him easily.

"Don't doubt that I want you, Jordie." Before Jordan could think clearly enough to speak, Trey continued. "Don't deny it. I could see it all over you. I was teasing you, and also being careful. You're as skittish as a colt. I didn't want to drag you straight up to the bedroom as soon as you arrived."

"You wouldn't have gotten any objection from me." Jordan barely recognized the sultry voice coming out of his own mouth.

"In that case." Without setting him back on his feet, Trey turned with Jordan in his arms and headed down the hallway. At the end of the passage, he shifted to reach the doorknob and swung the door open. He stepped over the threshold. The door crashed closed behind them. Trey relaxed his hold. Jordan slid deliciously against him. Feet barely on the floor, Jordan found himself spun around and propelled forward.

Trey sank onto the edge of the bed and pulled Jordan between his spread knees. "Kiss me."

Jordan looked down into Trey's hungry blue eyes. He could so very definitely do that. Leaning forward, he traced his fingers over Trey's lips and then along his cheekbones. Trey's eyes fluttered closed under the caresses. Jordan's fingers continued their journey, threading into Trey's dark hair. The thickly muscled body trembled.

"God, how I missed you." Jordan's voice echoed his reverence. His lips took possession of Trey's mouth, stifling any response. He nipped and suckled at Trey's mouth savoring the taste of his man until Trey pulled back.

"I need you to touch me, Jordie." Trey's shirt went flying as he ripped it over his head. Trey scooted back on the bed until he rested against the pillows. He crooked a finger at Jordan. He didn't need the invitation. Trey's naked chest made his palms itch with the need to touch. Jordan shucked his shoes, socks and pants. The tie followed the fate of Trey's shirt. He crawled up the mattress and straddled Trey's hips. Flattening his palms against Trey's perfectly etched six-pack, he remembered the first time he'd touched Trey.

He looked up to see Trey watching him. Banked fires simmered in his blue eyes. "I remember the first time," Trey said. "You took forever exploring."

"Because your body is amazing." Jordan's fingers began to move, tracing over the soft skin and hard ridged muscle. "There's more muscle mass now, but you feel the same." His fingers ventured higher, circled the tightened nipples. Jordan leaned forward and licked at one peak. Trey's big body bucked beneath him.

"Tease," Trey scolded.

"For now," Jordan agreed. For the next few minutes, he re-acquainted himself with the taste and feel of Trey's stomach, chest and throat. Trey's moans and curses were new. In high school, they'd had to worry about being caught so Trey had struggled to be quiet. Jordan hadn't been as successful, but alone in Trey's cabin, there was no one else to hear them.

Jordan's fingers slipped beneath the band of Trey's boxers intent on furthering his exploration. Seconds later, breathless and dazed, he stared up at a grinning Trey.

"It's my turn to play," Trey growled as he settled between Jordan's spread knees. "If you get down there, things are going to escalate rather more quickly than I'd like."

When Jordan offered no objection, Trey's hands stroked up and down Jordan's thighs before skipping over his boxer briefs to reach for the buttons of Jordan's shirt. The euphoria of being with Trey wobbled. He tried to relax. Trey had already seen the damage. He knew what lay beneath the cotton material.

The sides of the shirt fell away. Jordan fought the need to pull them back together. He looked up at Trey's face. Sadness and grief, tempered by love shone in Trey's eyes. No pity. No revulsion. Jordan's shoulders loosened.

"It would have killed me to see you injured and hurting." Trey's fingers shook as he stroked them over the scar tissue. "I can't imagine what you must have gone through."

"Don't think about it." Jordan shifted beneath Trey's gentle touch. "Not now. Just keep touching me." Jordan knew too well how easy it was to fall down the insecurity rabbit hole. He didn't want this time with Trey ruined by the past. "Please, Trey."

"You don't have to ask twice." Trey's hands and mouth got busy. Inarticulate moans and gurgles sang the song of Jordan's pleasure. He forgot the scars and the years apart. Trey's touch was as electrifying as he remembered. And, more skilled. The fumbling, hurried teenage approach had been refined to mind-blowing, erotic torture.

Unable to withstand the sweet torment without reciprocating, Jordan unclenched his fists from the sheets and reached up to grab Trey's hips. A demanding tug brought Trey's weight down on top of him. Pinned beneath the much larger body, Jordan strained to get even closer. He kissed and licked whatever he could reach while Trey's lips and tongue continued their assault on his senses.

When Trey pulled back, Jordan huffed his displeasure. Trey's chuckle snapped him out of lust's hazy grasp. Jordan blushed.

"You're gorgeous when you do that."

Jordan snorted. "I'm a long way from…"

"Stop." Trey brushed a swift kiss against his mouth. "Don't even go there. You are beautiful."

"The scars…"

"Show your strength," Trey interrupted again. "As I was saying, you're gorgeous when you're all flushed and aroused."

"But you stopped." Jordan couldn't believe he was pouting, but he was. He wasn't ready to stop.

"Because I need to be inside of you."

Trey's words, the look in his eyes, sent Jordan's heart rate into the stratosphere. "Then stop talking and get on with things."

Jordan lifted his face for a kiss, but Trey had other ideas. "Just lie back. I want to watch you."

While Jordan re-settled against the pillows, Trey leaned over to the nightstand and pulled out a drawer. Lube and condoms landed on the mattress at Jordan's hip. Condoms, plural. Jordan's breath hitched and stuttered. He raised up on his elbows.

"You're, umm, prepared." A flush stole up his cheeks.

"It's been a long time since I've had you. I'm a hungry man."

Heat raced through Jordan's bloodstream. He lay back against the pillows and lifted his hips. The boxers slid down over his ass and cock. He lifted one foot and then the other and they were gone. Trey's fingertips skimmed over his balls and then along the length of his cock. Strong, lean fingers closed around him. Jordan's hips arched into the tight grip. His fingers fumbled into the sheets until he found the lube.

"Hurry, Trey."

The hand on his cock disappeared. Warm lube dribbled over his ass. Trey's fingers soon followed, spreading the lube down his crack and around his hole. Pressure at his entrance brought Jordan's hips up off of the bed. Trey's finger slid inside to the second knuckle. Jordan's hips rocked riding the single digit.

"More." Jordan panted. "Harder."

"That's it, baby, tell me what you want." Jordan opened his eyes. Trey's big body loomed over him. He reached up and grasped a handful of Trey's wild hair. He pulled Trey down for a kiss and felt a second finger join the first. He bit down on Trey's plundering lips and then suckled the bruised flesh.

When the fingers slipped free, Jordan growled his displeasure. Trey chuckled. More lube drizzled over his ass. He felt the head of Trey's cock pressing against him. His eyes fluttered open and locked with Trey's stare. Trey's hips rocked forward. Jordan met him halfway as their bodies became one. They moved together in perfect rhythm. Trey's weight settled against him. Their mouths fused as tightly as their bodies.

The race to the pinnacle was even more beautiful than Jordan remembered. Fireworks burst behind his eyelids. Trey's murmured words of love the music his soul had missed. He flew higher and higher, his

J.T. Cheyanne

entire being wrapped around the man in his arms. Trey's hips slammed against his and his lover went still, body taut and straining as they fell over the precipice together.

Trey's arms gave out as the fall back to reality came. Jordan tugged him down loving the feel of Trey's body crushing him into the mattress. He clung to Trey as the tremors washed through both of them. He would never be able to let go again. Trey had always been everything to him. He was home and love and hope and family. He was where Jordan belonged and he was there again. Finally.

~*~*~

"Well, the top is a little bit crispier than it should be, but at least it's not burned." Trey laughed as he carried the lasagna pan in from the kitchen.

"I hope you don't mind, I did a bit of rearranging."

Trey paused and glanced around the room. Jordan had moved the low slung coffee table in front of the fireplace and covered it with a thick towel. A newly lit fire crackled and snapped behind the grate. Pillows from the sofas and chairs were tossed around the table for seating and two candles flickered in the center of the table.

"It's nice. Very Romantic."

When Trey's gaze returned to him, Jordan ducked his head, but not before Trey noticed the slight flush that stained his cheeks. Clearly self-conscious, he slid his hands in his pockets and shrugged.

"I like it."

A small smile pulled at Jordan's lips as Trey set the lasagna pan on the towel. He moved to slide an arm around Jordan's slim waist. When Jordan raised his head, Trey captured his mouth in a quick kiss. "I'll get the plates and silverware if you'll grab the wine."

After a quick trip to the kitchen, they settled in front of the fire. Jordan poured the wine while Trey dished up the food.

"I can't believe your team isn't having a coronary or something because you aren't practicing or going over plays or whatever. It's getting close to the end of the season."

"We lucked out not having a Christmas day game this year so I have a little extra time." Except, he didn't. He knew he should tell Jordan he had to leave early, but he didn't want to ruin the moment.

"I know I was hesitant about coming, but I'm glad I did." Jordan pushed his glasses up onto his nose, totally unaware of what he was doing as he thought about what he wanted to say next.

"There's so much I want to know."

"You can ask me anything, Jordie."

J.T. Cheyanne

Jordan looked over at him, smiled and did the bit with the glasses again. "Well, I was going to ask if you actually wore the underwear you endorse, but I found out that answer already."

"I do." Trey laughed at Jordan's flushed face. "But, like you said already, you know that. What else?"

"How did you meet Silas?"

Trey took a sip of the wine. "I met him the week of the draft. There were so many agents calling the school and dropping by the campus. It was chaos. All of them were making promises and dropping names. It was a huge headache.

"When I arrived at the venue on draft day, Silas was sitting in the lobby. In the sea of craziness, he gave the impression of calmness. He didn't chase athletes like the other agents. If players approached him, he talked to them. We made eye contact. His gaze wasn't predatory or speculative. It was honest and open. I signed with him that day, minutes before we were all ushered into the conference room."

"Sounds like you got lucky."

"I did. I wasn't his first client, but damn close to it. He's made me a very wealthy man."

"I think your talent had something to do with that as well."

"So, what about you? Why teaching and not an engineer at NASA?"

"Several reasons. Money was the main one. I got a settlement out of the wreck. My addiction blew through a lot of it. By the time I was sober, there was only about a third left. I received a few scholarships which helped.

"Time was another factor. I had wasted so much of my life. A teaching degree only took four years. A little less if I doubled up on classes."

Jordan adjusted his glasses. "The need for redemption. I needed to give back. I had been so lucky. I was alive. I had regained the use of my legs. I beat my addiction. There had to be a reason for my survival. And then, there was you."

"Me?"

Jordan looked across the table and smiled. "I remembered the many afternoons and nights I spent tutoring you. How good it felt when you were all excited about an "A" on a test. Teaching could give me the redemption I needed and in a loose way it kept me connected to the memories of you. Of course, actually teaching at Avery High definitely kept those memories alive."

"Wow." Trey didn't know what else to say.

They ate in silence for a while, each lost to their own thoughts. Eventually, the conversation turned to their stints in college and funny stories about co-workers and teammates. By the time the plates were empty and the wine was gone, they were both feeling pretty mellow.

"So, I um, brought you a present. Well, two actually." Jordan pushed up to his feet and retrieved two boxes from beneath the tree.

"I'll be right back." Trey dashed upstairs and grabbed the gifts he'd brought for Jordan. Back in the den, he found Jordan sitting on the sofa with the two presents beside him. Trey crossed the room and sat down on the other side.

"For you." He dropped a box in Jordan's lap.

"I didn't know what to get. You probably have everything already," Jordan said as he handed Trey the smaller box.

Trey opened his first. A bottle of Aqua Di Gio by Armani. "You remembered my favorite."

Jordan nodded. "You parents gave you some at Christmas our senior year. I think you used the entire bottle before we graduated."

"Not quite all of it, but I had a boy to impress. You seemed to love it," Trey teased. "Now open yours."

Jordan took his time unwrapping the box. He looked up with narrowed eyes. "Tickets to the playoff game."

"Yup, and since they are a Christmas gift, you can't and won't be paying me back for them. The airline tickets are in there, too."

"Trey, I can't..."

"Yes, you can. Consider it a gift for both of us. You get the tickets, and I get to have you at the game. I want you there, Jordan. You promised you'd come."

Jordan shook his head, but he was smiling. "Fine. You win. I'll be there."

"Now, the next one." Trey passed over the second gift, trying to hide his smile. "I think you'll like it."

Jordan took the package a bit hesitantly. "This better not be keys to a car or something."

Trey laughed. "Just open it."

A dark flush stole up Jordan's neck and heated his cheeks when he lifted the lid off of the box. His gaze snapped to Trey's face, eyes heated.

"I know how much you loved wearing my jersey back in high school. Thought you'd like a new one." Trey's voice emerged as a low growl. "I wore that one in the game on Thanksgiving. I can't wait to see it on you."

Jordan's lips parted. His eyes issued the invitation. Trey shifted to wrap an arm around his shoulders. It only took slight pressure to get Jordan into his arms. Lips met and clung. The banked fire in Trey's gut blazed anew. He groaned and pulled Jordan across his lap. Fingers tunneled into his hair. Trey shifted, tried to get them both horizontal.

"Wait," Jordan broke the kiss, panting. "One more. I have one more for you."

"It can wait." Trey dipped his head to run his lips along Jordan's throat.

"No." Jordan struggled to sit up. His hand slid along the cushions of the sofa. "I want you to have it. It's important."

Their hands collided and slid into the gift. Trey pulled it around in front of him and laid it on Jordan's thighs. He unwrapped it one handed as the other was trapped between Jordan and the couch.

The frame was simple, white distressed wood. The picture blindsided him as effectively as a middle linebacker. Jordan, him, the crowd. He remembered the moment as vividly as if it had been the day before.

"The championship game."

"I know." Trey brushed his fingers over the glass. He'd found Jordan in the craziness. He hadn't been able to kiss him like he wanted, but he hadn't been able to resist touching him. The photographer had caught the moment he'd lifted Jordan off of his feet. From the side, the camera had missed the love in his eyes and on Jordan's face.

"I have one just like that on my bedside table at home. Smaller actually. I stole it from the yearbook photo stash before we graduated." Jordan gave a slight smile. "And, it's the reason Carter figured out we dated. He saw it in the yearbook."

"Guess, he could see how badly I wanted to kiss you that night."

"He said it was the body language. You'd lifted me up, but you still held me against you instead of having your arms fully extended. That and the fact I had your phone number."

"Smart kid."

"He is." Jordan shifted.

"I love it. Thank you."

Jordan shifted. "I'm glad. Now, how about you kiss me and maybe later I'll model the jersey for you?"

"Sounds like a game plan."

Trey let the framed picture slide to the floor before he reached up to pull Jordan's glasses free. When he tapped his lips with the frame, Jordan pulled him closer and shifted lower in the sofa. When their mouths met again, the presents were forgotten.

~*~*~

Trey's phone rang late in the afternoon of the second day. In the process of making hot chocolate, Jordan snagged it off of the counter and carried it to the table where Trey sat.

J.T. Cheyanne

"It's Silas. You should probably answer it."

Reluctantly, Trey took the phone. He knew his agent would be calling with flight arrangements and he hadn't talked to Jordan about leaving early.

"Hey," he answered when the call connected.

"Plane leaves in the morning at 8 a.m. You'll be in Pittsburg by lunch. I'll pick you up."

"I'll be there."

"You better be," Silas ordered and immediately hung up, leaving Trey no chance to argue. Not that he planned to, he had a commitment to the team.

"You have to leave." Jordan stood across from him, holding his own mug of cocoa.

"Yeah, in the morning. Early."

"Okay."

"I'm sorry. I thought they'd give me more time."

Jordan shook his head. "It's okay. I can change my flight easy enough."

"You can stay here. Relax for a bit, watch the game on the big screen. There's plenty of food. Emmanuel can come back and take you to the airport."

"I don't think that's a good idea."

"Why not? It's my home. I want you to stay. You deserve some down time, and no one will bother you here."

"I'll think about it."

"Fair enough." Trey dunked a chocolate chip cookie in his cocoa. "So let's make the most of the rest of the day and night. Dinner tonight is on me, in town. There's a steak house you definitely need to try. Before that, want to take a walk around the property?"

"It's snowing out there." An objection, but Jordan was grinning.

"I promise to keep you warm."

"Who in their right mind could resist that temptation?" Jordan drained his mug and carried it to the sink. "I'll go ahead and warn you, I'm going to need lots of body heat."

"Is there another kind?"

Jordan laughed. "Come on then, you're wasting time."

Chapter Thirty
~ * ~ * ~

Jordan stared down at the field from his lofty position in the skybox. Somewhere in the locker room below, Trey was strapping on his pads and getting ready for the big game. Jordan had seen him very briefly when he'd arrived from the airport. While he watched, fans filed into the stadium like ants filling the empty seats. Advertisements flashed on the big screen. The field was a beehive of activity. Team managers, camera and sound crews, water boys or girls, they all rushed around making sure everything was ready for the first kick-off.

He'd seen it all before, on a much smaller scale to be sure. The only major difference between the professional playoff game and the two high school championships was the size of the crowd. He didn't know how Trey could tune it all out. The noise level would rise exponentially within the next half hour. The volume would remain at a steady roar for the remainder of the game. Secluded in the skybox, he would be shielded from the blare. On the field, Trey would be surrounded by it.

Turning away from the window, his gaze traveled over the luxurious accommodations of the private box. No hard benches and fold-out chairs in sight. Soft leather seats grouped around onyx marble-topped tables. Snowy linen napkins waited next to sparkling crystal glasses. Perfectly shined silver glinted from the overhead recessed lighting. A bar ran along the back of the wall with every type of top-shelf alcohol he could name and then some. Everything was a far cry from Avery.

He still couldn't believe how fast his life had changed. In the few weeks since Christmas, he'd been caught up in the whirlwind of Trey's nomadic lifestyle. Phone calls came at all hours of the day and night, rotating around practice, meetings with the coaches, photoshoots, and endorsement commercials; the list went on and on.

FaceTime and Skype kept things on a more personal level as in-person visits were simply not in the game plan. He had attended the last game, which the Wildcats won, and then Trey sent tickets for the playoff game that was about to take place below. There was no question he would be at the Super Bowl if that became a thing.

"And so, we meet again."

Jordan twisted around to face the door. Silas Barton, dressed smartly in a three-piece, charcoal gray suit stood on the threshold. He entered the box and closed the door behind him.

"Mr. Barton." Jordan dipped his head in greeting. "I missed you at the last game. Trey said you were busy."

Silas waved away the formality. "Call me Silas. No need to be so proper. We'll be seeing a lot of each other after all." He held out his hand. Jordan accepted the offer and shook. "I had another client making demands that his team wasn't thrilled about, but everything is all gravy now."

Completely out of his depth in that area, Jordan changed the subject. "Should be a good game today."

Silas glanced down at the field. "Let's hope so."

"Is Trey's contract in trouble? Because of me?"

"Not if he wins." Silas frowned. "I shouldn't have said that."

"It's okay." Jordan paced to the window and looked down. "I tried to stay away from him after you and I talked. I really meant what I said, but it's so hard saying no to him after hurting him thee way I did. Even though I stand by my decision, I can't help but feel like I need to make it up to him somehow."

"You did what you thought was best for him. I told him that."

Startled, Jordan spun around to face the other man. "What?"

"I need to apologize to you."

Jordan shook his head. There was no way Silas could know. Before he could stall the apology, Silas continued.

"First part, I'm sorry I came on so strong back in Avery about Trey's reputation and career. He was right. His personal life isn't any of my business."

Silas dropped his gaze. "As much as I wanted it to be." The other man shrugged one shoulder and then met Jordan's eyes again. "I wanted to tell you myself that I have…had feelings for him. I hid what I felt because I never really got the gay vibe from him. I was shell-shocked when I found him kissing you. And, so damn jealous."

"I'm sorry, Silas, you don't…"

"Just stop, this is my apology. You don't have anything to be sorry about, except for hurting him and that's between the two of you."

Jordan clammed up and waited.

"It's my fault for not speaking up. It's not usually my nature to hide who and what I am. And, I don't usually fall for my clients. Trey was different. He is different, but you know that." Silas scrubbed a hand over his hair. "It's pretty clear that even if I had voiced what I felt, it wouldn't have mattered."

The smile wobbled for a moment and then firmed.

"Anyway, second apology. I crossed every line in creation when I hired the P.I. to investigate you. I broke trust with Trey which I deeply regret."

Jordan's stomach dropped at the confirmation of his fears. "You did what?"

Silas actually blushed. "Ah, he didn't mention that to you?"

Jordan shook his head.

"Like I said; I was jealous and in a fit of temper, I hired an investigator. It was my hope he'd find some dark and dirty secrets I could use to convince Trey you were best left in the past."

Jordan felt the chill radiate out from his belly. He knew exactly what Silas had found. And it was every bit as dark and ugly as he'd wanted it to be.

"My plan backfired on me. When I read everything in that envelope, I knew I'd screwed up. Hell, I knew it within the first few pages. You told me you gave him up because you thought it was best for him. I don't' know how you did it. What you went through…"

"Stop." Jordan bit out the word. He didn't want the man's pity, and he certainly didn't want to rehash his tragic history.

"I invaded your privacy, Jordan, and I don't have any excuse for my abhorrent behavior. I'm sorry. The words seem inadequate but they're all I have to offer. I gave all of the information to Trey. I didn't keep any of it. I've tried to tell him to find another agent, but he won't listen."

Anger surged, but it was drowned out by humiliation. If Silas could find out about his past, others could as well. And if Trey came out, the media was bound to dig into his boyfriend's past. They thrived on gossip and scandal. They would come to Avery. The faculty would find out. All of it would be screamed across the news, across the world.

Jordan swayed on his feet. He could feel the panic attack crawling through him, and then he was sucked into the void. Breathing became a chore. His hands shook. The luxury box faded to white. Fingers closed around his biceps, pulled at him. Words floated in and out. None of them made sense. A loud banging echoed through his head. Voices arguing and then gone. Jordan closed his eyes and concentrated on Trey, bringing his face into focus in his mind. Deep breaths followed. He counted the ins and outs.

What felt like hours later, but was probably only minutes, Jordan opened his eyes. He was sitting in one of the leather chairs with his head resting against the back of it. The silence was only broken by someone's soft breathing. A single someone. He prayed it wasn't Trey. He was supposed to be getting ready for a ball game. Jordan lifted his head.

"Oh, thank God."

Silas.

Jordan swallowed his groan. "Sorry about that. Happens sometimes. I'm fine. You didn't, umm, you didn't call Trey did you?"

"No."

Jordan twisted around to find a sheepish expression on Silas's face. "He's getting ready for a game. A big one."

"Good call." Jordan pushed the rest of the way to his feet. He forced himself to hold Silas's gaze. "When the media finds out about me, is it going to hurt Trey?" There was no sense beating around the bush.

Silas was silent for a long time. "I think his coming out will be the biggest news. Your past will be a blip for him. He's used to the media frenzy. But you, it's going to be hell for you." Silas shrugged. "But, it won't be anything compared to giving him up. You went that route before. I understand the why of it, but I'm not sure I could have done the same thing. You have bigger balls than I ever could I'll tell you that. I'm not sure I could have been so unselfish."

Jordan blinked, surprised by the admission. "I turned into a drug addict. Nothing to be proud of."

"But you recovered, Jordan. You took all of the ugly life threw at you and turned it around. Yeah, you hit a few rough bumps, but you got up again, brushed all of the muck off your clothes and made a success of your life. When the media sharks start to circle, remember that. And remember this, Trey and I will be right there with you. You won't have to face them alone."

"You were wrong before."

Silas's eyebrows shot upward.

"Trey doesn't need to find another agent. He's got the best man by his side already."

Silas's shoulders visibly relaxed. A real smile curved his lips. "So, you aren't mad?"

Jordan considered for a moment and shook his head. "Anger won't solve anything. Trey is going to need you more than ever when he comes out. The more you know about the two of us, the better you'll be able to put a positive spin on it."

"I don't spin things." Silas exaggerated a shocked expression.

Jordan snorted. "You're an agent and a publicist. It's a wonder you don't sell tickets to your little merry-go-round."

Silas laughed and then grew serious. "Guess I better unlock the door and let the rest of the football wives into their lair." At Jordan's suddenly pale face, he laughed again. "What? You thought you'd have this thing to yourself?"

Chapter Thirty-One
~ * ~ * ~

Trey jogged to mid-field sparing a single glance at the scoreboard. They were down by a field goal, thirty-five seconds left in the fourth quarter and about sixty yards to the end zone. The Super Bowl loomed on the horizon. He dropped down in the huddle and met each and every one of the expectant gazes.

"They will be gunning hard for me." Heads bobbed. "But, I'm not going to have the ball. Erickson, I hope that throwing arm is still good." Jerrel Erickson flashed a grin.

"The triple F, yeah?"

Trey nodded. "Flea flicker fake. Castle, you get your ass down that line and get open. Linemen watch the scrimmage line. No illegals downfield. Stay in front of your defenders, no blocks in the back."

Trey nodded to Chase Newman, the center. He broke the huddle and took his place at the scrimmage line.

"Let's win this one, guys." The huddle broke apart. Linemen took their places. Darius Castle lined up far-right; Tyler Meeks, the other receiver took the left. Erickson took his place on Trey's right flank. Justin Finley, the fullback went in motion and stopped just behind the line on the left.

Trey took his place under center. "Red, thirty-six. Red, thirty-six. Hut. Hut."

The ball snapped into his hands. He rolled right, hit Erickson in the gut with the ball and snatched his hands back. He continued the run around to the left. He kept his arms tucked as if hiding the ball. The defense followed, fully convinced he had the ball. He pretended to stumble, felt the crosshairs on his back. The middle linebacker crashed into him just as he started to open up for the fake pass.

The crowd gasped. Trey twisted his head around to see the ball sailing down the field, a beautiful spiral pass. He held his breath along with the eighty thousand spectators. As effortless as breathing, Castle hauled the ball in and sprinted for the goal line twenty yards up-field. The defense scrambled, but Castle was too fast. He crossed the goal line with the closest man still five yards away. The stadium erupted.

Trey scrambled to his feet as their sideline emptied. Players streamed onto the field, shouting and laughing. Large bodies collided with him. Streamers and confetti rained down around them. Reporters swarmed the field. It was chaos, but the perfect kind.

His eyes swung up, up, up to the skybox where Jordan had watched the game. He lifted his helmet by the facemask and pointed it toward the box. Slowly, he brought it down to his mouth and kissed the top of it. A message to his man. He lifted it one more time in triumph before returning to the celebration on the field.

Microphones appeared from everywhere. Questions were flung at him. Some he answered, others he ignored. In the middle of the melee, he found himself dragged onto a makeshift stage for the presentation of the divisional championship trophy. More reporters with their cameras and microphones. Trey's gaze shifted to the skybox, his smile huge for the man there watching him.

When he finally escaped into the locker room, his teammates swarmed him. Congratulatory slaps peppered his shoulder pads. Smiles and laughter punctuated the high spirits. Somewhere a champagne bottle popped its cork.

Turning the corner to his locker, he glanced up and stumbled to a stop. Jordan stood near the bench in front of Trey's locker, trying desperately to look like he belonged in the midst of the rambunctious players. Erickson and Castle stood on either side of him, talking animatedly about the game.

Trey slid between them and did something he'd never been able to do after a game. He scooped Jordan up in his arms and spun him around. Trey grinned up at him. "We won."

Jordan's cheeks were bright red, but he smiled. "Yeah, you did. Congratulations."

"Do I get a kiss?"

Jordan's smile dropped. His eyes flicked around the room.

"They know, Jordie. I told them."

"Telling them is one thing; having a gay man in the locker room is something different."

"Just give the guy his kiss, dude. He earned it." Erickson winked and smacked Jordan on the ass. Trey felt Jordan's entire body jolt in response. He loosened his grip so Jordan slid down to his feet. Shielded somewhat by the bigger bodies, Jordan leaned in to brush his mouth quickly across Trey's lips. Not the kiss he'd wanted, but it was a huge step.

"Stay here, I'll go shower and we can all go out to celebrate." Trey pulled the shoulder pads and sweat-soaked jersey over his head. Heat flared in Jordan's eyes, and not of the embarrassed variety. Trey grinned, knowing all about Jordan's fantasies.

"I'll be quick."

~*~*~

Jordan watched Trey and his teammates disappear into the sea of bodies before sinking onto the bench in front of Trey's locker. He hadn't wanted to come down, but Silas had insisted. He'd been freaked out by the panic attack earlier and didn't want to leave Jordan alone. The agent had walked him straight to Trey's locker and told him to wait. Unsure of his welcome in the players' private domain, he'd taken a seat facing the locker.

Castle had been the first to acknowledge him. Erickson had joined them a few minutes before Trey's arrival. Both men had made an effort to put him at ease.

"Hey, we're all heading to STK for the post-game party. Tell Trey to meet us there." Jordan looked up to see a showered and dressed Darius Castle beside him.

"I will. Great catch out there."

The other man smiled. "Thanks. See you at the club later. I'll introduce you to my wife. You two can sit together next game."

"I'd like that," Jordan replied, still surprised at the easy acceptance.

"Later, then."

Jordan was just settling back onto the bench when his cell phone rang. "Janice! You won't believe where I am. The locker room. Trey's gone to take a shower and then we're going to some club called STK."

"Is there any way you can come home?"

Jordan's stomach plummeted. "Is Dad...what happened? Dear God, is he okay?"

"It's not your dad. He's fine, so is your mom. Jordan, I don't want to ruin your trip. I shouldn't have called, but he's asking for you."

"Who's asking for me? Janice, what the hell is going on?"

"It's Carter. He wanted to start the New Year with a clean slate. He came out to his dad. His dad, he didn't take it so well. He told Carter to get out. When Carter went to get his things from upstairs, his dad followed him. There was some pushing and shoving and...Carter fell down the stairs."

"Is he..." Jordan couldn't bring himself to say the words.

"He broke his leg and he was unconscious for a little while. The doctors say he has a concussion, but it's not too severe. He's scared. He doesn't have anywhere to go."

"Yes, he does." Jordan didn't even think about the decision. "I have a few spare bedrooms. He can move into my place."

"He doesn't have anything, Jordan. That's why they fought. His dad wouldn't let him take anything with him. He didn't even call the ambulance when Carter fell. Nika did." Nika, Carter's younger sister.

"Tell him I'll be there as fast as I can. Get mom or dad to go sit with him at the hospital if you can't."

J.T. Cheyanne

"Your mom's already here. She brought his school books. Apparently, she gave Mr. Lee a piece of her mind when she got them, but he wouldn't give her anything else."

"Mom's the best." Jordan's heart swelled with pride and love for his mother. She'd never once made him feel embarrassed or ashamed because of his sexuality. Carter had a new and powerful ally.

"You know where I hide the spare cash. If he needs anything, get it for him. I'll be home soon."

Jordan stared at the blank screen when Janice hung up. His thoughts shifted like hummingbird wings. He'd just agreed to take in a teenager, a student. Carter would need clothes and shoes and food and a bed and a computer. And those were just monetary things. He'd need a guardian, medical care, a therapist or counselor. They would have to go to court to make it legal.

The noises in the locker room broke into his thoughts. His eyes snapped up to the locker in front of him. He was just getting back into a relationship with Trey. What would he think? Jordan hadn't even discussed it with him.

"Jordan?"

He shifted on the bench to see Trey with a towel wrapped around his waist and his hair still damp. His easy smile dropped.

"I have to go home," Jordan blurted.

Trey went down on one knee beside him. "Your dad?"

Jordan shook his head and explained the call with Janice. Trey didn't interrupt, but the expression on his face darkened.

"That bastard needs his ass kicked. Carter deserves better than that."

"I agree. That's why I have to go home. I want to talk to the court in the morning. I want to try and get him placed with me. He doesn't have anywhere else to go."

"Jordan, that's a huge step."

"I know, but I have to do it."

"I'll do whatever I can to help you."

Jordan knew his shock showed on his face. "Really?"

"Absolutely. And, this makes me even more determined to come out. Kicking your child out because he's gay, that's total parent failure. I have a platform to expose him and other parents like him. Let me talk to Mr. Stromley and my Coach. I'm going with you even if it's just for the night."

Chapter Thirty-Two
~ * ~ * ~

Trey exited Coach Donahue's office and cut his way across the locker room to where Jordan waited at his locker. Stromley and Donahue had come through. The team jet was being fueled and made available. The Super Bowl game was two weeks away. They expected him back by Wednesday.

"Hey."

Jordan straightened on the bench. Questions danced in his eyes.

"We're a go. Stromley is letting us use the jet. We just have to get through the media circus waiting outside."

"Maybe I should go out the side door. I can meet you out front."

Trey wasn't having it. "We go together, Jordie. There's no reason to hide."

Jordan let him take his hand and guide him to the door, but just before they exited the locker room, Jordan let go and ducked through the double doors alone. Trey pushed through the doors. The crowd of reporters swarmed, effectively separating them. Microphones danced in his face. Questions rained down on him. Was he happy with the win? Stupid question. Would the win cement his re-signing with the Wildcats? Hardly.

Frustrated, he tried to push his way through the crowd to get to Jordan, but the sea of cameras and reporters refused to budge. With the doors at his back, he had no way to escape the inevitable. He held up his hands for silence.

"I'm sorry. I know you all have questions, but I don't have time to answer them. My friend…" He paused as the media sea shifted and he caught a glimpse of Jordan. He stood alone against the wall, arms crossed and head down. The media ignored him; he was invisible to everyone but Trey. For some reason, that pissed him off.

Trey shoved at the crowd with more force. He broke free of the mob and faced Jordan. He held out a hand. Uncertainty danced in troubled light brown eyes. Jordan scanned the room at Trey's back before his eyes dropped to Trey's extended hand. It seemed to take an eternity, but Jordan's fingers twined with his own. Behind him, the room went silent.

Still facing Jordan, Trey resumed speaking. "You all don't know him, but Jordan Brooks is a high school teacher back in Avery where I grew up. One of his students was kicked out of his own home and attacked earlier today simply because he's gay. I'm taking my fiancé back to Avery so he can make arrangements to protect this child and take him into his home. So, if you guys will excuse me, we have a plane to catch."

J.T. Cheyanne

The ensuing roar was deafening. Trey felt a hand on his back. Silas's voice filled his ear. "Go, I've got this. The car's waiting outside."

"I'm sorry, Si. I know I was supposed to wait."

"We'll deal with it. Now go."

Tugging Jordan by the hand, Trey hurried to the exit. True to Silas's word, the limo waited at the curb with the motor running and the back door open. He shoved Jordan inside and tumbled in behind him. The limo was away from the curb before he righted himself in the seat.

"What did you just do?" Jordan demanded, eyes wide and shocked.

"I believe it's called coming out." Trey leaned forward to open the mini-fridge. A bottle of champagne sat in ice. He snagged it and then two glasses.

"I got that part." Jordan moved to the edge of the seat and stopped him from opening the bottle. "I meant the other part. The fiancé part. You know my parents were watching the game. Your parents too. We haven't even discussed marriage. We just decided to start dating."

Trey smiled. The look of shock on Jordan's face was priceless. "You are so wrong, Jordie. We have discussed marriage. In depth. Surely, you remember all those nights we spent under the stars while you planned out the perfect ceremony. I certainly remember them."

"But, so much has happened since then," Jordan sputtered.

"Have you changed your mind? You don't want to marry me?"

"No." Jordan shook his head. "I mean yes."

Trey's smile shifted to a full grin. Jordan was absolutely gorgeous when he was flustered. He reached up and snagged Jordan's glasses, and tapped his lips with the frames. Jordan automatically leaned forward. Their lips brushed briefly before Jordan pulled back and glared at him.

"You did that on purpose," he accused. Trey wasn't about to deny that accusation. It thrilled him that Jordan still responded so quickly and without consciously thinking about what he was doing.

"We'll be at the airport in about fifteen minutes if you want to call your mom before we board."

"And tell her what exactly?"

"That we're engaged. Weren't you just a part of that conversation?"

"Trey, I'm not sure…"

"About what? Did you want the bended knee thing again?" Trey slid off the seat and dug in his pocket. "I was going to do this after the game anyway, but shit happens. It always does between us." The small velvet pouch finally came free. He dumped the contents on his palm. Jordan sucked in air.

"You still have those?"

J.T. Cheyanne

Trey looked up into disbelieving toffee-colored eyes. He shrugged, not in the least embarrassed. "Of course I have them. I told you that last night we were together I'd keep them safe until we could put them on together."

Jordan emitted a laugh sob combination. "But, you said you hated me when I didn't show up."

Trey shook his head. "I said that I tried to make myself hate you. I was never very good at that. Anger could muster in spades. Why do you think I stayed away from Avery?"

At the puzzled look on Jordan's face, he shook his head and smiled. "I knew that when I saw you I'd either kiss you senseless or turn you over my knee and beat your ass. Either way, I wouldn't be able to keep my hands off of you."

Trey dropped his head and fiddled with the rings in his hand. "It was clear something had changed your mind. I didn't want to force anything on you. For a long time, I hoped that you would come find me. And then, pride put an ugly boot in the race. I refused to run back with my tail between my legs, so to speak. But, I did accept every endorsement sent to me that I knew would air nationally. I wanted my face on your TV screen. I wanted you to remember me. See me on that screen and wonder what if."

Trey's fingers closed around the rings. "Not a pretty sentiment is it."

Jordan slid across the seat until their thighs touched. Gently, he pried Trey's fingers open. One by one, he transferred the rings into his own palm before picking up the larger one to stare at it.

"So many nights in that hospital, I lay in the dark and made plans to go after you. I played it out so many different ways. In some you were angry, some you were happy. In all of them, I walked into your arms."

Jordan stopped talking and swiped at his cheeks. "When the recovery took so long and I couldn't walk, the depression swooped in and wiped out everything except the pain. That's when I started taking the pain meds. I'd avoided them for so long. But, they eased the pain, not just in my body but in my heart. Oblivion was better than knowing what I couldn't have."

"We both made some pretty dumb mistakes."

"Yeah, we did." Jordan laughed. "Your plan worked, you know. Every time I saw one of your commercials, especially the underwear ones, I'd lose focus on whatever I was doing and stare at the TV. I may or may not have bought several dozen packages just because your face was on the package."

Jordan turned Trey's hand over. The ring slid on his third finger easily. "There. That's where it was always meant to be. I'm sorry, Trey. Sorry that I wasn't stronger. Sorry that I turned away from you. Sorry that

I didn't believe in your…our love. I do want to marry you. More than anything."

"I hear a 'but' coming."

"I'm going home to possibly adopt a teenager. I'll have to go to court and who knows what else. Carter's probably going to be angry. He'll need counseling. Teenagers are moody and difficult at the best of times. Are you sure you're ready for all of that?"

"With you? Yes."

"You do realize you just came out to all of those reporters. You're going to have to deal with the fallout. What if they void your contract, or try too? You'll have a fight on your hands. On top of that, you want to tackle the legalities of foster care?"

Trey blew out a frustrated breath. "Jordan, stop overthinking and listen to me. I want you in my life. I want to marry you. I want to make up for all of the years we've missed. I know it seems sudden, but it's not like we just met."

He shook his head when Jordan tried to speak. "I'm not saying we have to get married next week, or even next month, but I've been waiting for you since the day I left Avery. I was going through the motions of life, a side character in my own story because it was easier to follow the script than to step up into the breakout role."

"This isn't a rom-com, Trey. It's real life."

"It's real now because I found you again."

Jordan huffed and then held his hand out, fingers spread wide. "When you put that ring on my finger, it's for keeps. I won't let you go again."

Trey eased the ring along Jordan's finger and over the last knuckle. "You won't ever have too, Jordie. I've always been yours." Trey brushed a tender kiss against Jordan's lips. "Now that it's official, call your mom."

Chapter Thirty-Three
~ * ~ * ~

"Hey, baby." Jordan's mother stood and enveloped him in a hug. "Congratulations to the two of you. It's about time." She repeated the hug with Trey. "You played a great game. Sorry, we had to drag you away from the celebration."

"It's okay. I'd planned to skip out with Jordan anyway. I had this question I intended to ask him followed by a different sort of celebration." Trey's heart-dropping smile flashed. Jordan felt the flush rise from his toes to paint his cheeks crimson. He reached up and shoved his glasses further up on his nose and cleared his throat. His mother laughed before turning to face the sleeping teenager on the bed.

"He tried to wait up for you, but the pain medication knocked him right out."

"Is that safe? With a concussion?" Jordan moved around his mom to stand at the bedside. Trey circled the bed to stand opposite. Jordan's heart broke for the kid. Carter looked extremely pale and very young against the white sheets. A vivid bruise marred the right side of his face. Beneath the blanket, the stark outline of the cast testified to the demons Carter had faced.

"The nurses are keeping an eye on him and I've been here with him since Janice called me."

"Thank you, mom. I appreciate it."

"He's family now; we take care of our own." She looked up at him, face fierce. "His father needs a swift boot to the ass. He should be ashamed of himself. If he dares show his face in church on Sunday, I'm going to give him a piece of my mind again."

"It won't do any good." Jordan dropped an arm around her shoulders. "He has us now, and we'll take care of him." Jordan didn't add that Carter was one of the lucky ones. So many of the LGBTQ youth didn't have anywhere to go.

"Why don't you head home and check on dad. Trey and I will stay the night with him."

"Not happening. Trey just finished a football game and you both had to travel. Your dad is fine at home. Janice is keeping him company."

"What about the diner?"

"It's closed due to a family emergency. I want it clear to these people in Avery that we support you, Trey and Carter. I'm not ashamed of my son and his family."

J.T. Cheyanne

Love for the woman standing in front of him thickened his throat. Jordan hugged her again. "Tell him we stopped by and we'll see him after we meet with Family Services."

~*~*~

Jordan parked and stepped out of the warm car. He shivered in the icy air. There was no sign at the road but the GPS said the nondescript, one-story, brick building was their destination. Snow crunched underfoot as they walked toward the door. A sign against the glass confirmed their destination.

"You don't have to go in." He turned his head to look at Trey.

"When the season ends, I'm going to be living with you. I think that little detail will matter."

Jordan flushed, shoved his glasses up on his nose and reached for the door.

"That's number fifteen since we left Avery," he heard from behind him followed by Trey's soft chuckle. Warmth stole through Jordan. He stalled in the entry forcing Trey to stumble against him in the small space.

"You're going to have to stop counting in here. I'll be nervous so I'll probably fidget with them a lot."

"Then you should have worn your contacts."

"You like the glasses," Jordan answered without thinking.

Trey's large hand slid over Jordan's hip and applied the slightest pressure. "Yes, I do. I like the kisses even better, but I'll behave in here. I know this is important to you."

Jordan nodded and reached for the second door into the actual office space. Heads popped up from behind computers. A gasp sounded to his right, telling him Trey had come in right behind him.

"I need to talk to someone about becoming a foster parent, or adoptive parent. I'm not sure of the process." He caught himself reaching up to adjust his glasses and dropped his hand.

No one moved for a few seconds. A woman who appeared to be around his mother's age finally stood up from behind her desk.

"We can certainly help you with that." She gave the room a hard stare. Heads dropped back down behind computers. She approached with her right hand extended.

"I'm Samantha Hughes."

They shook hands. "Jordan Brooks. I live in Avery."

"Come have a seat and we'll start the ball rolling." Her eyes flicked over his shoulder. "Will your fiancé be applying as well?"

Jordan shouldn't have been surprised. Every sports page in America was abuzz with Trey's declaration after the game the day before. It had been on the radio as soon as they had touched down in Wyoming.

Reporters had swarmed the airport. There had even been a hearty few to sleep in front of his house through the night.

"I, uhmm…"

"Yes, I will." Trey's arm came around Jordan, uniting them. "That won't be a problem will it?"

"Not at all, Mr. Bright."

Two hours later, Jordan stood in the small entryway with a headache, a fistful of papers and a court order granting him temporary emergency custody of Carter. He would receive a court date in the mail for a full-fledged hearing.

"That went pretty smoothly."

Jordan nodded, but his eyes were fixed on the crowd of reporters milling around on the other side of the door. "I don't think this is going to be as easy."

Trey's eyes flicked over the media and he shrugged. "It's part of the territory. You'll get used to it. Just put your head down, don't comment no matter what they say and walk straight to the car. Don't hesitate. They're like vultures; they'll scent blood."

"They wouldn't be here if you'd done exactly that after the game." Jordan shot Trey a glare which he totally ignored.

"We were going to have to deal with them at some point."

Jordan sighed and shoved his glasses into place. Trey was right. At some point, the media would have become an issue. Better to just get it over with and move forward.

"Let's go then. I know Carter will be waiting to see us."

Trey took his hand. The door swung open and they were in the midst of chaos. Jordan tucked his head and followed Trey through the mass. Questions rained down around them. Trey never slowed his pace. The car door swung open. Jordan slid into the passenger seat and reluctantly let go of Trey's hand. Seconds later, Trey sat beside him. The horde parted to let them pull onto the road.

"You think they'll follow us to the hospital?"

Trey nodded. "Probably, but security should keep them in the lobby at least."

"We're going to have to warn Carter. And, what about the foster situation? I can't even share pictures of him on social media, I definitely can't have his face plastered all over the news."

"He won't have to face them," Trey said. "We'll figure out how to get him away from there without being exposed to them. He's been through enough with his dad. When we get to the hospital I'll call Silas and have him release a brief statement asking for privacy. We don't have to give any details."

Jordan subsided into the seat and let Trey concentrate on the icy roads. His thoughts tumbled one over the other. Trey needed to be with the Team. The biggest game of his life, of his career, was less than two weeks away. He should have been focusing on the game plan. Instead, he was in Wyoming dodging a media minefield. He doubted Trey would listen if he tried to convince him to go back to the Wildcats.

"Stop worrying, Jordie." Trey's big hand moved to cover Jordan's where it lay against his thigh. "Everything is going to work out."

Jordan wasn't so sure.

Chapter Thirty-Four
~ * ~ * ~

Jordan rounded the corner headed to Carter's room and stopped short.

"Mom, dad!" Trey skirted around him and approached his parents. Hugs were exchanged. "What in the world are you doing here? I thought you were living up the beach life."

"You get engaged and you think we're going to miss it?" She laughed and patted Trey's cheek. "We're so happy for both of you."

Faced with Trey's parents, Jordan's insecurities reared their ugly heads. He caught himself shoving his glasses up his nose and quickly tucked the offending hand into his pocket. He stared a hole in the floor desperately wishing there was a way to escape into Carter's room. How much did Trey's parents know? Were they upset with him? Did they think he was too damaged for their perfect son?

Lost in his doubts, he didn't notice Caroline Bright's approach until her arms were around him. "Welcome to our family, Jordan. It does a mother's heart good to see her child happy and loved."

Jordan blinked in surprise. His eyes focused on her face. There wasn't anything negative in her expression, just love and happiness. Jordan hugged her back and dared lift his gaze to meet Allen Bright's eyes. The older man stood with an arm around his son's waist.

"We're here for the two of you. We'll do all we can to help you with Carter. I will warn you," he said with a sparkle in his eyes. "Your mothers have done nothing but talk wedding plans all morning."

Trey groaned. "Really, Mom?"

Caroline laughed. "Well, I won't have my only son getting married by a justice of the peace. I want a real ceremony and so does Tavia. I know you don't know the difference between a petunia and a daisy, much less what kind of cake needs to be served."

She looked at Jordan. "And, your mother was very clear that if it didn't involve numbers and equations, you were clueless." Jordan flushed and nodded. "Right, so you two will leave everything to us with free access to Trey's bank account."

"Wait, I'm paying for this?" Trey feigned horror. "I thought parents paid for the wedding."

"Not when your child is a multi-millionaire," Caroline shot back.

Jordan's face lost all color. He felt the blood drain all the way to his toes. Trey probably earned more in a single game than he did in an entire year. He couldn't let Trey pay for everything. It wasn't fair. He needed to figure out how to cover his share. Maybe a loan?

"Jordan." Trey's face swam into view. A frown marred his handsome features. "What's going on in that head of yours? You went ghost white."

"We need to have a prenup signed. I'll pay for my share of the wedding. I'll get a loan. I have good credit. Or maybe, a mortgage on the house."

"Stop right there, Jordie. There's not going to be any talk at all about a prenup. I refuse to even consider it. And, you most certainly will not get a loan to pay for anything."

"I'm sorry. I didn't mean to cause a problem." Caroline's face bore a look of distress.

"It's okay, mom. You didn't." Trey never broke eye contact with Jordan. "He's going to have to get used to the idea that we have money. We. The two of us. Not me. Us."

Jordan didn't know what to say so he kept his mouth closed; lips pressed together tightly. His nod seemed to satisfy Trey and he finally turned again to face his parents.

"Let's go see, Carter." A strong arm slid around Jordan's hips and tugged. He leaned against Trey and took a shaky breath. He hadn't asked Carter what he wanted, but he hoped the teenager would be happy with his decision to seek custody.

"Let me, um, maybe I should go first." Three pairs of eyes turned his way. "He just lost the only family he's ever known. He's hurting and scared. Everything is overwhelming and hard to take in. Believe me, I've been there.

Trey took his hand, linked their fingers and squeezed. A quick kiss brushed across his mouth. "I'm here for both of you. Let me know when he's ready."

~*~*~

Trey shoved his hands into his back pockets as Jordan disappeared into the hospital room. The night and day since the playoff win certainly hadn't gone as he'd planned. He didn't regret a single moment of it. Lying beside Jordan the night before in the house they'd dreamed about so long ago, he realized he'd come home.

"You okay, baby?" A small hand pressed against the small of his back. His mother rested her head against his bicep.

"Better than I've been in a long time," Trey answered. "I know its cliché, but it's like a giant boulder has been taken off my shoulders."

"Weren't you supposed to wait until the season was over?" His father handed him a cup of coffee. "The team isn't going to hold this against you are they?"

Trey took a sip of the hot brew. "I don't care if they do, dad. The contract is signed. If they choose to void it, I'll deal with it however Silas and his legal team see fit. But, I chose football over Jordan the first time. I won't do it again. He is my future. Carter is, too, if the courts agree to let us have him."

"You're taking a big risk. What if you don't get to play again?"

Trey looked at his dad and shrugged. "I'll be disappointed. Probably angry. My home life shouldn't have any bearing on my professional career. It sucks that it does. But, at the end of the day, I'll have Jordan, a man who loves me, the real me, not the persona the world has always seen."

"As long as you're happy, that's all we want." His mother chimed in from his side.

"Trey?"

He looked up to see Jordan standing at the door of Carter's room. He motioned for Trey to come with him.

"We'll be out soon," he assured his parents and went to Jordan. "How is he? Is he okay with going with us?"

"I think he's in shock. He wants to see you."

Jordan stepped aside to allow Trey to enter the room. Propped up in the bed, Carter didn't look quite as pale as he had the night before. Tear tracks marred his cheeks. His fingers twisted in the light blanket. The cast on his leg ignited the anger deep in his gut, but Trey didn't hesitate. He went straight to the bedside and sat in the empty chair. Carter didn't look at him.

"Mr. Brooks says I'm going to live with him. And you."

"That's the plan if you're okay with it."

Carter looked up startled. "If I'm okay with it?"

Trey nodded. "We want to help you, Carter. To give you a safe place to live. But, if that's not what you want, we can figure out another way to help you."

Carter's eyes fell back to the blanket. Silent tears slid down his cheeks. "I know I wasn't supposed to, but I told my dad you're gay. I thought it would change his mind. He laughed in my face and called me a liar."

The weight that had been removed from Trey's shoulders returned with a vengeance.

"I'm sorry." Again, Carter's eyes flew up to meet Trey's gaze. "I wasn't as brave as you are."

"Brave?" Carter sneered. "More like stupid. I shouldn't have said anything. I knew better."

"Just listen, okay." Trey moved to the edge of the chair and held his gaze steady on Carter's tear-streaked face.

"Twenty years ago, I let my fear win. I chose to stay in the closet to protect my secret so I could play football."

"And now you're rich and famous. And not homeless."

Trey checked his temper at the boy's father and reached across to take Carter's hand. "That's all true, but I lost something very precious. I lost Jordan." He extended his other hand to Jordan. When the other man took it, Trey pulled him closer.

"Two homes, a fat bank account, trips to exotic cities. It all sounds amazing, and it is. Except, I was all alone. I left my heart and soul right here in Avery because I was scared to admit who I really am. Because I kept quiet, I didn't know Jordan was in a terrible accident and almost died. I missed twenty years that we could have spent together."

"It wasn't your fault," Jordan interrupted.

"I have to own my share of the blame," Trey answered. "I could have left campus to come back and check on you. But, that would have opened me up to a lot of questions that I didn't want to answer. So, when I tell you that you made a brave decision, Carter, I mean it. It took a lot of courage to come out to your dad. I'm really sorry things went badly for you. I'm especially sorry that my lack of courage played any part in what happened to you."

"What if he tells the newspapers?" Carter's hand trembled in Trey's grip. "I could get you in trouble."

Trey laughed. "Well considering I told the national news last night that Jordan is my fiancé, I don't think the local news is going to have much of a scoop."

Carter's eyes went saucer wide. "You did what?"

"It's all over the news, trending on Twitter and Instagram, too."

"My dad smashed my phone."

"We'll get you another one."

"I don't understand." Carter's wounded expression tugged at Trey's heart. "Why do you want me when my own dad doesn't? Mr. Brooks knows me, but you've never met me."

"Because you're brave and smart. Because you need to know that there are people in the world who will love and support you unconditionally. Because I don't want you to be a statistic, the gay, homeless kid who committed suicide. And because you remind me of my Jordan when he was your age."

Carter didn't speak. Instead, he pulled his uninjured knee up to his chest, rested his head on his crossed arms and cried. The heartbroken sobs tugged at Trey until he got up and sat on the bed to drape an arm around

Carter's thin shoulders. Jordan circled the bed and sat on the opposite side.

"You aren't alone, Carter." Jordan rubbed the boy's back. "You've got us for as long as you want us."

Chapter Thirty-Five
~ * ~ * ~

"Trey! Over here."

"Trey, how long have you known you're gay?"

"How does your sexuality affect your contract? Are the Wildcats renewing?"

"Why haven't you come forward before now?"

"Is your team comfortable with you in their locker room?"

The barrage of questions drowned out the noise of the busy city and game-day traffic. Reporters jostled against them as Trey and Silas tried to get from the limo to the stadium entrance. A microphone poked through the melee and collided with Trey's chin.

He growled and tried to break the iron grip Silas had on his arm.

"Not now," Silas breathed into his ear. "You need to stay focused on the game. Security's coming, they'll break up this craziness."

Four burly guards waded into the crowd and created a buffer zone around Trey and Silas. Head high and eyes straight ahead, Trey crossed the rest of the distance to the entrance. Instant silence surrounded them when the doors clicked closed behind them.

Trey rotated his shoulders and exhaled long and slow. "Are Jordan and Carter on the way?"

After the heartbreaking visit with Carter, Trey had kissed Jordan goodbye, hugged his parents and headed back to the airport. With the Super Bowl on the horizon, he had to get back to his team. He'd talked to Jordan every night after practice and team meetings were over, but it wasn't the same as having Jordan right there with him. After the twenty-year separation, he hated having any distance between them.

"Yeah. Family Services cleared the trip and the doc okay-ed the flight. They should be landing shortly after lunch. I'll meet them at the airport and bring them here."

"You have to avoid the media. They can't take pictures of Carter."

"I know the rules, Trey. I'll take care of your guys. I've never let you down, have I?"

Trey smiled. "No, you never have. I'm sorry I let you down."

Silas waved away the apology. "We're past that, remember? I'm fine. I'm going to take a page from your book and come clean with the world. There's going to be speculation about the pair of us."

Trey shrugged. "Let them think what they want. As long as you and I are good, I don't really care what they think. Not anymore."

"And Jordan?"

J.T. Cheyanne

"I think you made it clear to him there was never anything between us. He told me about the panic attack."

"I didn't mean for that to happen."

"I know, that's why I didn't fatten your lip for you."

Silas grinned. "You really love him."

"I do." Trey dropped his own smile. "Even if it means giving up football. I want to be with him. I've always wanted to be with him."

"We're going to try and make sure you don't have to give it up. Winning this game will definitely help." They split with a fist bump at the entrance to the locker room. "Good luck out there."

~*~*~

"We'll send Carter in with your parents. No one knows who they are. I have someone on the inside waiting to meet them and take them to the skybox. Mr. and Mrs. Bright are already there. You and I will brave the media and provide a distraction. You sure you're up for this? They can be pretty blunt."

"I saw what happened when Trey arrived. Surely, it won't be that bad for me?"

Silas shook his head. "You're in the spotlight now so yeah, it will be. I can try to figure out another way to get you in?"

Jordan shook his head. "I'm not going to hide from them. This is part of Trey's life and I have to get used to it. This is the biggest night of his professional career so why not start now?"

"You know they'll all be looking for a scoop; the more devious ones will be looking for dirt."

"Yup, I know. After that panic attack in front of you, I talked to my old therapist, my parents and Trey. I've shared some of it with Carter. The people who matter to me already know the ugliness. They still love me. I have a support system to catch me and stand me back up again. I can do this."

"Okay then, let's get you guys inside." They rejoined Carter and Jordan's parents. Silas shook his dad's hand.

"We're going to the stadium in separate vehicles. The media is expecting to see Jordan. They'll be hungry for a glimpse of Carter, but we need to avoid that for legal reasons. Mr. and Mrs. Brooks, you'll be taking Carter with you. This is Kelly, my PA." A slim young woman joined their group.

"She'll take you three to the stadium in my car while I take Jordan in the limo. Hopefully, we will draw all the attention our way. Kelly, when you see them swarm us, get those three out of the car and into the stadium. You're cleared with security."

Turning back to Jordan, he winked. "Time to be the offensive line." Jordan looked at him mystified. "We're going to block the quarterback." He pointed at Kelly. "And, make sure the ball gets away safely." His pointing finger swerved over to Carter.

Jordan actually grinned. "I can do that." Reaching into his carryon bag, he pulled out Trey's white game jersey he'd gotten for Christmas and tugged it over his head. Without the shoulder pads and Trey's added bulk, it fell almost to his knees. "He left this for me to wear."

"Marking his man." Silas chuckled. "That will definitely work."

The ride to the stadium passed in a blur. Emmanuel lowered the glass separating the driver from the rear area. "As soon as I get out, they're going to be all over us. They know I'm Trey's regular driver."

"It's okay, Emmanuel," Jordan spoke up. "We need to keep them focused on us."

Emmanuel nodded and raised the glass before exiting the limo. In seconds, the passenger door swung open. Jordan took a fortifying breath and stepped out into pandemonium. Trey's jersey shone a blinding white in the sunshine. Silas quickly joined him and began the process of moving forward against the rush. Questions peppered the air. Cameras whirred. Microphones performed their one-legged dance in the air above their heads. Jordan ignored them all and kept his eyes focused straight ahead.

"How does it feel to know you've single-handedly ruined Trey's career?"

Jordan stopped. Silas's hand landed on the small of his back and tried to move him forward. He could hear the man frantically whispering in his ear. Jordan turned to face the man who'd thrown out the infuriating question.

"I haven't done anything to Trey except love him. If his career is ruined, that's in the hands of the team owners and the league. I can't control that. And, if you're referring to the fact he's gay, well that's on God, so you can take your accusations to him. Trey is the same man today he was when he was leading this team to the Super Bowl. Nothing's changed except your pathetic attitude."

He glared at the man until Silas strong-armed him forward. Other questions rained down around them, but Silas didn't give him another chance to stop. When they finally gained entry to the stadium, Silas released him and stepped back. Jordan expected a dressing down; instead, the agent was grinning at him.

"So, the teacher has fangs after all."

Jordan flushed. "Maybe we should make sure Carter got in okay."

Silas chuckled. "Okay, this way."

J.T. Cheyanne

They wound their way around to an elevator. Silas hit a button and the silver doors slid open without a sound. Inside, he hit a floor and then entered a code.

"What happens if he loses this game?" The question hung in the air between them.

"First, he can't lose the game by himself. It's a team sport and you can bet your ass I'll argue that point. We both know Trey is going to go out on that field and play just as hard as he ever has. His ability will not be in question.

"Second, the contracts are already signed. If they want to void them, they'll have to pay him a hefty sum. He hasn't done anything wrong, except for spilling the gay beans a bit earlier than they would have liked."

"You seem pretty confident."

"I've had my legal team go over and over the contract. Even had a civil rights specialist go over it. If Trey gets cut and wants to fight it, we'll fight. It won't be easy on him in the locker room if the players don't back him, but he can handle himself."

"This is exactly what I tried to avoid twenty years ago." Jordan circled his hands around in the air. "All of this media circus and the homophobic bullshit."

"I know Trey doesn't agree, but you probably made the right choice. Even if they didn't yank his scholarship, he wouldn't have been drafted. The world wasn't ready to accept him. You had the foresight to see that."

"Only after I got hurt." Jordan stopped talking when the doors swished open. They found the hall empty. He stepped out and glanced over at Silas.

"That's not true exactly. I worried about it all the time. I tried to talk to Trey about it, but he just brushed it aside. I don't think our relationship would have survived even the four years of university. I'm not sure I could have maintained my silence if I'd been with him every day."

"Maybe, maybe not, but it's in the past. You have him now, and whatever comes you'll handle it together."

"Yeah, we will. Thank you, Silas."

The agent stopped at a set of double doors. "I told Trey this morning; I'm going to come out too. It won't draw any heat off of him, but it may cause more. You know there will be speculation. I want you to be clear that nothing ever happened between us."

"Even if it had, we weren't together then. You're a good man and you've been a great friend to him. You took care of him when I couldn't. For that, I'll always be grateful."

"Friends?" Silas stuck his hand out. Jordan ignored it and went for a hug instead.

J.T. Cheyanne

"Definitely, friends." He stepped back. "Now, let's watch some football."

J.T. Cheyanne

Chapter Thirty-Six
~ * ~ * ~

On the sidelines next to his head coach, Trey's attention switched between the field and the time clock. Forty-five seconds. No time-outs left. The Siberians' quarterback came to the line. Fourth and five, on the Wildcats' twenty-yard line. A touchdown and two-point conversion could tie the game. The Wildcat defense spread wide across the field.

The strong safety bounced on his toes at the ten-yard line angled to the quarterback's right side. His throwing arm. The free safety hovered around the five-yard line, about center of the field. The quarterback's knee came up. The ball snapped into his hands. He dropped back and surveyed the field. The entire stadium seemed to hold its breath as the ball sailed into the air.

The wide receiver broke away from the strong safety, eyes on the ball. He leaped upward and caught air. Jaques Minnifield, the free safety, knocked the ball away. The arena exploded with sound. Fans screamed in victory and defeat. The announcers yelled into their microphones. The Wildcat sideline erupted in euphoric shouts.

Trey spared a quick hug for the coach and hurried onto the field. There was enough time for one snap. He knew they would take a knee, didn't need to see the offensive coach for the call. They didn't bother with a huddle. The line scrambled into position. Trey took his place under center. The play clock wound down seconds ahead of the game clock.

"Hut, hut!" The ball came at him like a bullet. He tucked it into his chest and hit a knee. The buzzer sounded. Electrified chaos exploded around him. His own line tackled him. Hands slapped him on the back, the helmet and the ass. Elated voices rang in his ears. Trey hugged the game ball to his chest, stared up at the domed ceiling and grinned. They'd done it. Super Bowl Champions. A lifelong dream come true. And somewhere, up in the skyboxes, Jordan was there.

~*~*~

Jordan watched the last seconds tick off the clock. The crowd counted them down. When four zeros appeared, Carter rocketed out of his chair, hopping on the one good leg, yelling and pumping a fist in the air. His parents and Trey's parents hugged, cried and laughed. Fierce pride flooded Jordan. At long last, Trey had achieved his dream. The Wildcats were victorious.

Joyful tears dampened his eyes while a lump fueled by pure pride threatened to choke him. He fought the need to rush out of the room and find Trey in the melee below. He wanted so badly to wrap his arms around his man and congratulate him.

J.T. Cheyanne

"Come on, I'll take you to the field."

Jordan peeled his eyes away from the swarm on the field to look at Silas. How did he know? He wanted to go. His entire body felt like he was attached to a live wire. His gaze darted to Carter. He couldn't risk the teenager being caught on camera.

"We'll stay here with him." His mother and Caroline spoke simultaneously. "Go." His mom shooed him toward the door where Silas waited.

"Get the kiss this time," Carter teased, making both women laugh.

Jordan flushed, shoved his glasses up on his nose, and finally grinned. "Yeah. I think I just might do that. I'll see you guys in a bit." If his eagerness showed on his face, he didn't care. He just wanted to get to Trey.

He dashed out the door after Silas. The other man must have been familiar with the stadium because they were on the field in less than five minutes. Celebratory chaos created a dull roar as players were interviewed, announcers were giving game stats, other players were celebrating, and fans screamed from the seats. He had no idea how Silas intended to find Trey.

A hand clamped down on his forearm. Silas tugged him through the fringes of the crowd, avoiding the reporters and cameras. Jordan realized he was steadily working his way toward the stage hastily set up in the middle of the field. He caught a glimpse of Trey's jersey and then it was swallowed up in the sea of elbows, cameras and shoulder pads.

A sharp whistle cut through the rumble of voices. Jordan stumbled into Silas when the man stopped suddenly in front of him.

"Sorry," he mumbled while shoving his glasses back into place. A sudden silence brought his head up, eyes wary. They landed on his man, standing about a yard in front of him in full pads. Jordan's heart knocked hard against his ribs as Trey's entire face lit up with his smile.

Trey's helmet hit the ground. Flashbulbs popped and flashed. Trey moved swiftly through the disco effect until Jordan found himself hauled close to a sweaty jersey. The familiar scent of "football player" filled his nose. He looked up into Trey's brilliant eyes.

"Congratulations," he breathed seconds before Trey's kiss landed on his lips. Stretching to reach above the shoulder pads, Jordan wrapped his arms around Trey's neck and returned the kiss with all the love bubbling inside of him. He didn't care about the cameras or the reporters. His guy had won the biggest game of his life.

"I love you." He couldn't contain the words when they broke apart.

J.T. Cheyanne

Trey spun him off his feet, his smile wide. "I don't know how you got on the field, but I'm glad you're here." Another kiss followed. "We won!"

Jordan grinned back at him. "I know. I was watching. You played a great game."

"Okay, I've held them off as long as I can. Several reporters want to talk to you." Silas tapped Trey's shoulder pads and then pumped a thumb over his shoulder.

"So, you brought him." Trey chuckled as he hugged his agent and friend. "Thank you."

"Part of my job." Silas winked. "Congrats on the win."

"Thanks."

"But seriously." Silas jerked his head toward the milling crowd.

"Yeah, yeah. I've got it."

Jordan tried to sidestep along with Silas and slide away, but Trey grabbed his hand and laced their fingers together. Suddenly, it wasn't so easy to ignore the cameras and microphones.

"Now that you've won the Super Bowl what are your plans?" The first reporter, a CBS affiliate, asked.

Trey's megawatt smile flashed. "I'm taking my guy to Disney World, of course." Jordan forced a smile as the camera panned his way.

"And will you be returning to the Wildcats next year? Has your coming out affected your contract?"

Jordan's heart plummeted to his stomach. So much for game talk. Trey's fingers tightened around Jordan's hand, but his smile never faltered. "Coming out hasn't affected my ability to play football. In truth, it's been easier to play knowing my truth is finally out there. As for the rest, you'll have to talk to the owners and the coaches. The contracts were signed last month. I'll play as long as they want me, to."

"Winning the Super Bowl will certainly help. Congratulations."

"Thank you."

Jordan watched the CBS guy move on to another player as a different reporter stepped forward to question Trey. "Congrats on the win." Trey nodded. "Fans were worried when you took off after the big reveal following the playoff game. There was some concern that you wouldn't be focused for the big game. I don't think that was an issue today."

"Not at all. I knew that Jordan was taking care of everything at home. If there was a problem, he would handle it, or he'd let me know he needed me."

"He has some experience watching you from the sidelines."

J.T. Cheyanne

That wasn't a question, rather, a statement of fact. Jordan dropped his gaze to the grass avoiding the camera's all-seeing eye.

"Yup. We were dating when I won the championship in high school my senior year."

The reporter seemed surprised Trey answered the question, especially honestly. He seemed to debate the next question. Jordan breathed a sigh of relief when he went with the game topic.

"You threw for three hundred and ten yards, three touchdown passes and ended up with four hundred and sixty-eight yards total offense. Were you trying to prove a point?"

"I didn't do all of that by myself. We have great receivers and running backs and none of us could move the ball if the offensive line wasn't doing their job. We played as a team and thankfully, luck was on our side tonight."

"Did everything work out for the student?"

Jordan froze when the microphone was shoved in his face. Trey squeezed his hand. He caught himself reaching for the glasses and shoved his free hand in his pocket. He wasn't quite brave enough to look into the camera so he held the reporter's gaze.

"For the most part, yes. Physically, he's safe and has a safe place to live. Emotionally, it will take time. He's having to adjust to a new reality, but with counseling and a good support system, we're hoping he'll find his foundation again."

"We wish him the best." Jordan thanked the man and was very glad to see him leave.

The third reporter stepped forward and attention again focused on Trey. Jordan barely resisted a relieved sigh.

"Congratulations on the win."

"Thanks."

"Are you disappointed that you didn't win the MVP trophy? Do you think it has anything to do with you coming out last weekend?"

"No, I'm not. Castle deserved the win. That one-handed catch in the corner of the end zone was beautiful. I overthrew him a bit, but he hauled it in. I don't think my coming out had anything to do with the voting, but if it did, so what." He lifted their joined hands and kissed Jordan's fingers making him blush again.

"I got the best win in the world right here."

"Apparently, you got that win all the way back in high school?" Jordan's stomach flip-flopped. Why couldn't they just ask about the game?

"I did and wasn't smart enough to hold on to it. But, I've got it now."

"Care to elaborate?"

J.T. Cheyanne

"Watch the documentary. It's airing tomorrow night on ESPN, special feature," Silas broke into the conversation and handed Trey his dropped helmet. With a practiced move, he insinuated himself between the reporter and Trey explaining the documentary and effectively allowing them to slip away.

Chapter Thirty-Seven
~ * ~ * ~

Sitting on the edge of the mattress in their hotel room, Trey thumbed the remote to turn the volume up. His own face filled the screen. Off camera, Silas had been asking him questions; about his high school years and the donation check, the footage of which had aired earlier; about his college experience and then about his professional years. None of that had mattered to him as much as the part coming up next.

Jordan sat beside him. Their parents spread out behind them on the king-size bed. Carter sat on the floor on his other side. Silas sat at the table, flipping his phone over and over in his hand while waiting for any fallout.

"Why did you decide to come out now, at this point in your career?" The onscreen Silas asked. Jordan's palm slid over his thigh as the camera panned in closer to Trey's face on the television screen. Trey dropped his head as his onscreen persona started to speak.

"Because denying who I was, who I am, cost me twenty years that I can never get back with the man I love. Because when I reconnected with him at the reunion, I realized that I had chosen, by default, to keep my secret hidden. In doing so, I never knew that he almost died trying to come to me after we graduated high school."

Soft gasps from their mothers spilled into the room at his back. Tears stung his eyes. He reached for Jordan's hand and threaded their fingers together. Thank God the video continued.

"We dated secretly our senior year. As you saw in the video, I was the small town quarterback, in the paper every Saturday morning after the game. Every man and boy in Avery knew who I was, the local standout with a shot at something huge. But, none of them knew the real me. Not even my own dad."

Jordan leaned into him, dropping his head onto Trey's shoulder as the on-screen Trey chuckled. "Even then, Jordan didn't hide who he was. Brilliant, focused on his studies, especially math, and gay. He never said that word, but all the kids knew it. A few of our classmates, including some teammates, picked on him. One day, I'd had enough. I wasn't brave enough to come out, but he lived his truth every day.

"I defended him that day behind the diner to everyone's surprise. And then, I needed to know how he did it. How did he ignore what everyone else thought about him?

"Away from the school bullies, he wasn't the awkward and shy boy everyone thought they knew. He intrigued me. I asked him to tutor me in

Calculus just to be able to spend more time with him without people figuring out my secret.

"It worked. I fell for him. So hard. I found myself thinking about him instead of going over the playbook. I skipped out of practice early so I could study for non-existent tests. I counted down the days to graduation when we could leave Avery and share a dorm room, away from everyone who knew us.

"I left and went to summer practice at the university. Jordan was supposed to join me there, but he never showed up. I thought he'd changed his mind, decided to go to MIT instead and study for the job he wanted so badly with NASA. He wouldn't answer my calls. His parents stonewalled me. I was devastated. I couldn't focus. A coach told me to let go of the past and I used that excuse to get angry and ignore the twisting in my gut.

"I resisted going back for the reunion. You forced my hand." Through the television, Silas's laugh erupted into the silent room. The televised Trey shook his head and continued. "I saw him leaving the school the day I presented the check. It was a sucker punch from Fate. I thought he was gone, that I would only have to battle the memories.

"I have to apologize to everyone at the reunion. I was there, but I wasn't. I searched for him all night in the crowd. Needless to say, we found each other again. My anger and hurt demanded answers. I wasn't prepared for them, and he wasn't very eager to share. It took a few months, but I learned Jordan hadn't abandoned me, not in the way I thought he had. He was hit by a drunk driver, burned severely and paralyzed."

The television went silent. Trey kept his head down. He knew that onscreen, he was fighting tears. Carter's hand circled his calf and squeezed. Jordan's body shook beside him.

The televised version of himself found his composure and continued. "In horrible pain, terrified and unsure of his future, he made the decision to let me go. He wanted me to have my dreams, to live the life I'd planned instead of being tied to a broken shell of the boy I knew.

"Everything I thought I knew about myself vanished that night. I wasn't a role model for the kids out there. I wasn't someone for them to look up to and admire. I was a coward. While he suffered through recovery, I was hiding behind my helmet and shoulder pads. I never once considered leaving campus to check on him. I didn't want anyone to know my secret."

"And, that's why you're here now?"

"Yes. To tell the world, I am a gay man. A gay athlete. It doesn't change the man you've known. It doesn't change the stats I've put up. It doesn't change how I play the game. It shouldn't change what anyone thinks about me. But, it will. And, it doesn't matter. The one thing that matters most to me right now is for the world to know that I love Jordan Brooks and I intend to marry him just as soon as he agrees."

The brash jingle of a commercial rang out as the documentary faded to black. No one moved or spoke. Trey held his breath. Were his parents upset? He'd told them the truth already, but were they hurt he hadn't told them in high school? And what did Jordan's parents think? Had they blamed him like Janice had?

Jordan cleared his throat. "Mom, Mrs. Bright. You have about a month to pull this together. I don't think I can wait any longer to marry him."

The bed pitched and rolled. Arms went around them. Kisses and hugs were pressed everywhere. Happy tears washed away the hurt and anger that had been festering for too many years.

"I wish you had felt safe enough to tell us back then, baby." His mom.

"We wanted to tell you, but Jordan was so adamant that we couldn't." Jordan's mom.

"We'll have the reception at the diner." Mr. Brooks.

"I love you, son." Softly, in his ear from his dad.

And through it all, Jordan was there beside him, their hands tightly clasped.

Silas cleared his throat. He and Carter stood to the side, slight smiles on both faces. "Commercial's over." He cocked his head toward the television where his face came back on screen.

"The last part of the documentary has been pre-empted. I believe Trey announced his engagement following the playoff game. And, as this is being filmed prior to the Super Bowl game, I would like to make it very clear that win or lose, the owners, coaches and players for the Wildcats intend to keep Trey as their quarterback and fully support him and his fiancé as they embark on this new chapter in their life. Congratulations to the two of you and thank you to everyone for watching."

Stunned, Trey stared at the TV and then at Silas. His agent nodded and gave him the thumbs up. His gaze drifted around the roomful of people he loved most in the world. His eyes stopped when they landed on Jordan. His beautiful brown eyes shone with pride and love.

Trey struggled to grasp the extent of his good fortune. He'd won the Super Bowl. His job wasn't in jeopardy. He was surrounded by family and friends. The loneliness that had been a constant companion since leaving Avery was gone. Love and acceptance filled every nook and cranny inside of his soul. Pure joy seemed to circulate in his veins.

J.T. Cheyanne

Trey tugged Jordan closer by their joined hands. With exquisite care, he brushed his mouth across Jordan's full lips. A sense of peace settled around him.

"Now you can tell me I'm living my best life," he whispered when he pulled back.

"How about I just say, I love you?"

"Works for me."

"I love you, Trey Bright. I always have."

THE END

J.T. Cheyanne

DISCOVER OTHER TITLES
BY J.T. CHEYANNE

~ * ~ * ~ * ~

Grand Slam

Ocean's Kiss

Ansleigh's Grotto

Collateral Damage

COMING SOON: Innocent Man